Running with Mother

Running with Mother

by

Christopher Mlalazi

WEAVER
PRESS

Published by Weaver Press,
Box A1922, Avondale, Harare. 2012
<www.weaverpresszimbabwe.com>

Typeset by Weaver Press
Cover Design: Danes Design, Harare
Printed by: Sable Press, Harare

ISBN: 978-1-77922-187-2

Christopher Mlalazi, who is currently a member of the Iowa Writing Program, was the Nordic Africa Institute 2011 Guest Writer in Uppsala Sweden. In 2010 he was the Villa Aurora Guest writer in Los Angeles, USA. Prolific as a prose writer and playwright, in 2008 he was the co-winner of the Oxfam Novib PEN Freedom of Expression Award at the Hague for theatre, and in 2009 was awarded a NAMA award for his short story collection, *Dancing With Life: Tales From The Township*. He was nominated for another NAMA for his novel 2009 novel, *Many Rivers*. In 2010 he won a NAMA for his play *Election Day*.His latest play *Colors of Dreams*, also opened to a full house at HIFA 2011.

Chapter 1

My school is just too far away. But like it or not, it's the only secondary school among the four villages in the Saphela area of Kezi district.

Although it's far away, the school is easy to find. You just follow the big Saphela road – which was recently built and cuts through our village of Mbongolo – and it will take you right to the gate of Godlwayo Secondary in the neighbouring village.

Before the new road was built, there was a winding strip track. The old road now runs beside the new one sometimes crossing and recrossing it like a drunk person. Both these roads pass in front of my home at Jamela Bus Stop. Jamela is my family name. I'm Rudo Jamela.

Few cars travel down either the old road or the new one. Uncle Ndoro's bus does so in the late afternoon every Friday going towards Godlwayo and the other villages beyond; on Saturday mornings it returns towards Bulawayo where my father works and lives.

There is also Mr Donga's old lorry. He's the owner of Godlwayo Store near the secondary school; he has another store in Mbongolo, which is next to the primary school. His lorry is very rickety and when you see it, you can't help but smile. It travels up and down between his two stores with supplies. Sometimes, if we're lucky, Mr Donga gives us a lift, but when we're too many he just hoots and shouts, 'Too many!' as he drives past. That's why his nickname is 'Too Many', but I don't think he knows.

***

It was a very hot afternoon, the kind mother says can take fish out of water. We were walking back from school on the narrow footpath that winds between the two Saphela roads, and approaching the S-bend, which is the halfway mark between home and school. I was with my cousin Sithabile, and my two friends Nobuhle and Belinda – we're all in Form 2B – and we were all in our green school uniforms with cream belts. I was walking in front with Nobuhle. She's the daughter of Headman Mabhena in Mbongolo village, and she's a tall attractive girl, already with breasts like an adult, not like me. I'm a very short girl – too short for my age, which is fourteen – I can easily pass for a ten-year-old. Sometimes it's good when people underestimate my age, as I can get away with things like punishment at school, but sometimes my classmates call me 'Shortie'. Usually, I don't mind unless someone means to ridicule me. Mother says one day I will catch up with all the others, but I don't believe her. Anyway, my father is a short man, so maybe I take after him.

Belinda is a neighbour, the daughter of Sibanda, who's the Headman's messenger. Sometimes he doubles as the village policeman, even though he sells beer from his home.

I was thirsty. We had drunk some water from the school borehole before we left, but it was so hot that I'd become thirsty again. Fortunately, a little way ahead, was the Mbongolo Primary School borehole and we planned to drink from it. Mbongolo Primary is not far from my home, and where I did all my primary education.

***

The golden rule when walking a long way is not to look ahead: just focus on each step at a time. But today we'd broken that rule because the sky was filled with smoke. We had already passed Donga's store in Godlwayo. Belinda had been the first to see it but we'd not taken much notice because controlled fires are common in spring as people prepare their fields for planting and sometimes burn all the shrubs they've uprooted. But as we left Godlwayo village and entered Mbongolo, a dark fog seemed to hang over the whole village like a bad omen.

'I think it's a bush fire,' Nobuhle said. 'There's too much smoke for

2

somebody to be clearing their field.'

Bush fires are not taken lightly. A few months back, our headmaster, Mr Ndlovu, had told us at assembly that some part of Lotshe village – which lies to the east around the Phezulu mountains – had been destroyed by a fire started by some boys smoking mbanje. Although no one had lost their lives, he'd warned us that we must never play with matches or fire.

Without realising it, we'd left the footpath and were walking as fast as we could down the big new road. Deep down, we were all anxious about our families. I was in front as I'm faster than the others – I'm the one-hundred-metre-sprint champion for the under-fourteens at school, a title I won last month, just before my birthday.

'A car's coming,' I heard Sithabile say. Ahead, toward the approaching S-bend, a column of thick dust twisted towards the sky. 'Are you sure it's not a whirlwind?' I asked, as I couldn't hear an engine. Whirlwinds are also common in spring. It's fun to chase after them as they race through the village.

Nobuhle pressed her ear to the ground. I followed suit. The earth was hot against my cheek.

'Is it a bus?' Belinda asked.

'No. It must be Too Many,' Sithabile said.

'It can't be,' I interjected. 'I saw his lorry parked behind his store.'

'Make a guess, then, Rudo,' Nobuhle said, 'What is it?'

Guessing the make of a car from its sound was a game we often played when we were walking along the road. Whoever wins is titled Nkosikazi and everyone claps hands for her.

This vehicle, whatever it was, had still not appeared and the dust cloud was thicker than ever, as if a giant broom was sweeping the road.

'Not a bus,' I said. 'But a tractor.'

The sound, which was deep as a bus, seemed somehow different, as if it was straining. But I was wrong. It was the bus. It appeared at the bend, and we all watched it in astonishment. It was racing like never before. Behind the bus, in the distance, rose another cloud of dust, suggesting that there was a car behind it.

We quickly got off the road and onto the grass. The bus raced towards us, and the dust cloud chasing behind it seemed like the upraised tail of an angry cat. The bus was yellow and had a red stripe down the middle, so we knew it belonged to Siyahamba Bus Service, the company Uncle Ndoro drives for. Strangely, its roof carrier was empty. It's usually piled high with goods when it's coming from the city, especially at month end. Then, suddenly, the bus seemed to veer from side to side, as if blown by a strong wind, although there was no wind, just the hot sun shining.

We watched mesmerised. Then the bus turned and skidded towards us, broadside on, like a person's feet sliding in sand. Then it leapt into the air. I was aghast. Everything was happening too fast.

The bus turned around once like a spinning brick in mid-air and bounced back on the ground on its wheels, bounced again, and then veered to the side and bounced off the road and into the bushes as something large and dark seemed to fly out of its front window.

It slammed sideways into a tree and with a groan came to a stop like a tired man who's been running too hard. The top of the tree fell over the bus, like a sheet placed over a corpse.

The noise of the crash hung in the air.

In shock, we clung to each other, scarcely believing what we had just seen and heard.

Chapter 2

Everything seemed to freeze. A large cloud of dust slowly settled on the road and, as it did so, a figure emerged. Completely covered in dust, it looked like a ghost, but it was Uncle Ndoro. He was holding his head in his hands, and his face was raised to the sky. Silently, he limped across the road and disappeared as if he were an apparition.

I know Uncle Ndoro well. He calls my mother his sister even though they're not related, because they both come from the village of Chisara in Mashonaland East. So, like family, he calls my father his *tsano*, and me his *muzukuru*.

As soon as Uncle Ndoro disappeared into the dust cloud, I looked at the bus. A thick column of smoke was now pouring from its front, adding to the dust still clouding the air above it.

We were rooted to the side of the road, helpless, not knowing what to do. Then I found myself pulling away from the other girls and taking a step towards the bus. I imagined it full of people, one of them my father. He always comes to the village at month end – though for some reason he had not come the previous month. Then I figured that he wouldn't have been in the bus as it had already passed our bus stop. But perhaps the bus had not stopped – it had been travelling so fast.

My father had written to me (Uncle Ndoro had delivered the letter) saying that he would bring me a surprise present for winning the running championship. In my heart I had hoped for white boxer shorts, like a proper athlete.

As I took a step forward, Sithabile pulled me back just as the dust cloud cleared, and my heart skipped a beat as I saw an army truck full of soldiers with red berets parked at the side of the road, parallel to the crashed bus. It seemed as if it had arrived by magic because the accident had absorbed all our attention.

The soldiers stared at us. A shiver of fear ran through me. We were all suddenly afraid, very afraid. In the front seat beside the driver was a man with many badges on his chest, who wore a camouflage cap on his head and large reading glasses. He was smiling at us. Seeing his smile, I shrugged Sithabile's hand off my arm and stepped towards the army truck.

'The bus has just crashed,' I was shouting at the soldiers. 'There might be passengers inside; the driver ran off that way.' I pointed in the direction in which Uncle Ndoro had stumbled.

The soldiers just stared back at me nastily. No one moved. None of them looked at the bus, and then I felt their eyes shift to the girls behind me.

The passenger door of the truck opened, and the smiling officer jumped to the ground.

'What are you saying, girl?' he asked me in Shona.

'The bus crashed,' I replied in Shona.·

The smile of the soldier changed into a frown. I had never seen a soldier wearing reading glasses before, sunglasses yes, but not reading glasses, and the ones this solder wore almost made him look like a school-teacher, even though there was a pistol tucked into the holster at his waist.

'You speak Shona?' he asked abruptly. I nodded my head.

'What's your name?' His smile was back but his voice was stern.

'Rudo.'

'Your surname?'

'Jamela.'

'Why do you have a Shona name and a Ndebele surname?'

'My mother is Shona.'

'And your father is Ndebele?'

'Yes.'

The soldier looked at the three girls behind me. 'Do your friends speak Shona too?'

'No they don't.'

'Tell them to come nearer.'

I called my friends. Then the soldiers at the back of the truck, about nine of them, jumped down to the ground. I noticed that at the back of the truck was a man whose upper body was tied with rope, fastening his hands to his side. He had a black sack covering his head. There was something familiar about him, which I could not put my finger on, but I felt it would come to me at any moment.

The girls drew nearer apprehensively. I looked at the soldier in the reading glasses. His eyes were on them. He was still smiling. Then he held his hand out in front of him, and a soldier placed a parcel in it, which was wrapped in silver foil, the action so fluid it had clearly been done many times before. The soldier unrolled the parcel, took an object from it and dangled it in front of us.

I felt my heart lurch and I heard the girls behind me gasp in horror.

It was a human hand. It had been chopped off at the wrist, which still glistened with blood. I noticed the flash of a silver ring on one finger.

Chapter 3

Sibanda, Belinda's father, has a party trick, which, when I first saw him perform it, frightened me so much I nearly ran away. I was in Grade Five then. Sibanda had just brought Belinda to our school. She had been to school in the city, but the aunt with whom she had been living had just died, so she'd to come back to the village. Till then I had only known Sibanda from a distance as he ran errands around the village for the Headman; and, of course, Auntie sometimes visited Sibanda's home to drink his homebrew.

That day, when Sibanda brought Belinda into our classroom, our teacher had told us to stand and greet him.

'Good morning Mr Sibanda,' we'd chorused. Instead of replying, Belinda's father had opened his mouth and of all things for an adult to do, he'd stuck his tongue out at us. And on the tip of his tongue was a row of teeth. A shockwave spread round the classroom. None of us had ever seen a tongue with teeth before. The man had then plucked the teeth from off his tongue and held them up to the class, baring his lips to show us that he had no front teeth. Without his teeth, his face seemed to deflate like a plastic ball that someone has stepped on.

'If you listen to your teacher and get well educated,' he lisped, 'you won't lose your front teeth like me. These are plastic teeth that I bought in the city after somebody knocked out my teeth in a street fight.'

Then he fitted his teeth back into his mouth, and suddenly his face looked younger again, and the class had all laughed and clapped their hands.

* * *

'This is the hand of your Headman Mabhena,' I heard the soldier tell us in English. His smile grew wider, as if the fact pleased him.

Nobuhle began to scream. The soldiers had surrounded us, so we were imprisoned inside a tight ring of men in camouflage uniform.

The front of the bus had begun to burn and the smoke turned black and acrid.

I didn't want to believe what the soldier was telling us. I tried to pretend that he was just playing, like Belinda's father and his false teeth. Nobuhle's father was a very important man in the village, a man who was respected, who tried crimes and meted out punishment to all those found guilty. What kind of a crime could he have committed to have his hand cut off as punishment? I had never heard of such a thing.

Maybe the soldier was fooling with us, wanting to frighten us, and what he'd shown us was just a rubber hand, but then I remembered that Nobuhle's father always wore a silver ring, a small cow's head with fiery red eyes fashioned into the band. It had always fascinated me. Nobuhle told me that it was not a wedding ring but one that her father had bought in Bulawayo because it symbolised the value of his cows in the village.

I was lucky that day, but my friends weren't.

The officer holding the dead hand shook it at me.

'You,' he said in Shona. 'Hurry, disappear, and don't look back. This is a matter for the Ndebele people only.'

Nobuhle and the other girls were now grabbed by the soldiers, as if they were also going to have their hands cut off. Nobuhle was still screaming.

'I'm travelling with the other girls,' I said, and received a resounding clap that knocked me onto the ground, the boot of the officer just beside my head, his figure looming large into the smoke-filled sky. From where I was lying, he looked as if he had two right hands.

I quickly got up and ran away. The girls screamed behind me. A short distance away, and despite the warning, I darted a look over my shoulder, and I felt as if cold water had been thrown in my face. The girls were naked, without underwear. The soldiers must have torn their school uniforms off, as I saw them lying on the road, though one was hanging forlornly on a bush. As I looked back, the soldier in the reading glasses raised his hand, there was an explosion and I found myself lying on the ground for the second time that afternoon.

'Get up!' I heard the soldier shouting. I got up. The soldier was still pointing at me. I did not feel injured. He must have missed me. I remembered my mother once saying that during the war of liberation if a person heard a gunshot that meant you were still alive.

The other soldiers were dragging the naked girls into the bushes beside the road. I left the road and ran into the bush, my heart in my mouth and my feet flying, and headed in the direction of my home. Screams followed me.

But I didn't run far. I don't know what came over me that day: maybe it was the screams. I hate screaming. I also felt that by running away, they wouldn't stop, but if I stopped they would also stop. So as soon as I was out of sight of the soldiers, I found a thick bush and dived underneath it. I could still hear the screams, and I wanted to cover my ears, they were so piercing, and so full of dread, as if the girls were now having their hands cut off like Nobuhle's father. I felt sick.

Finally, after a long time, the screams stopped, and there was silence. Then I heard the sound of a car starting and driving away and I knew it could only be the army truck.

Chapter 4

I lay on my stomach under the bush as the sound droned off into the distance. I could see a bit of the road, but not as far as where I'd left my friends. I could also see the column of smoke from the burning bus rising above the bush, and I knew I would be able to see the girls walking home down the road.

A long time passed, I guessed about an hour from the angle of the shadows, but there was still no sign of life. My eyes were still focused on the road as if I could conjure my classmates into being.

I was also on the look out for Uncle Ndoro. I wished that he would reappear and bring sense to whatever was happening, as he was the only other adult besides the soldiers who had been nearby. Right now, the only other person who could give me protection was my mother and she was still a long way away and didn't even know what had happened to us.

I noticed a movement in the short grass. It was a hare and it was approaching my hiding place. I had lain so still that it hadn't yet detected me. It chewed on the grass in rapid bites, casting quick glances around it, but not in my direction. The bush seemed deathly quiet – well, the crickets were trilling as usual, but there was no other sound.

The bush I was hiding under was a *skhukhukhu*, which has leaves that are silver underneath and green on top. You can stick them together to make a mat to slide down rocks; you can even make a guerrilla hat from them when you are playing in the bush.

The hare suddenly darted towards me; maybe it wanted to get under my bush, maybe the sun had suddenly become too hot for it, or maybe its warren was somewhere nearby; and then it stopped and looked about. It was a gentle little animal. I wanted to reach out and touch it as it looked towards me with shiny brown eyes as if it had been aware of me all along and was just playing a game with me.

Please little animal, I found myself praying and looking directly back at it. Please tell me if it's safe to come out.

The hare cocked its head to one side and then the other as if it was deciding what to do, and I coughed. The sudden explosive sound caught me unawares and the hare shot off in the direction of the road. I cautiously stood up. If the hare had run in that direction, there were surely no people there – but where were the girls?

I walked towards the spot where I had left them, moving carefully from bush to bush beside the road. Even though I knew that the soldiers had gone, part of me remained very afraid.

I finally reached the crashed bus. The flames that had engulfed it had died down, and only a trail of bitter smoke emerged from it. The tree it had smashed into had been reduced to embers. Fortunately, it had stood in a clearing of sand, so the surrounding dry bush had not also caught fire.

Suddenly I froze. A figure had materialised from the other side of the road. It was not wearing an army uniform. It was Uncle Ndoro. He walked over to the bus and stood beside it, giving no indication that he had seen me, although I was in plain view. I watched him closely. Slowly looking over and around the bus, he disappeared for a moment. He seemed not to have noticed me, which was strange in itself and somehow made me afraid to call out.

I walked towards my uncle as he reappeared on the other side of the bus, and as I did so, my heart filled with relief. The school uniforms and underwear that had been lying scattered on the ground had disappeared: I hoped this meant that the girls had dressed up and left – maybe they'd taken a bush path so as to avoid meeting any more soldiers.

'Were there any passengers in the bus, *muzukuru wangu?*' I heard Uncle Ndoro ask me when I reached him. He spoke in Shona.

Uncle Ndoro is of medium height with a slight body; he was wearing blue overalls, which were still covered in dust, as was his hair and face. I had heard the story of how he came to be driving for the yellow Siyahamba Bus Services, deep in the heartland of Matabeleland, so far away from Chisara, from my mother. At first he had driven buses in Chisara; then he had decided to go to Botswana to earn *mapura* but he had no passport, so he had been quickly caught by the police and deported back to Rhodesia, as the country was called then. He had decided to stay in Bulawayo and prepare to return to Botswana. Instead, he had fallen in love with and married an Ndebele woman, MaTshabalala; so he had found a job driving buses to Kezi for Siyahamba Bus Service. Later MaTshabalala had died and left Uncle Ndoro four children, whom I sometimes see when I visit father in the city. There are two boys, Thabani and Kudakwashe, and two girls, Tapiwa and Sibongile. My father's house is in Lobengula Township next to the community hall where films and weddings are sometimes held.

***

I looked at Uncle Ndoro. I was baffled. He was wringing his hands like a confused child, with a low keening sound. With a shock, I noticed that blood was still trickling down the right side of his neck and into his overalls.

'I don't know. I didn't see inside the bus before it crashed. … But are you okay, Uncle Ndoro?' He didn't sound okay to me.

'I've forgotten if there were any passengers,' Uncle Ndoro answered, taking me further by surprise. His eyes were glazed and he appeared not to recognise me, though he seemed to know that I was still a child. 'Please tell me.' And he sighed heavily, like a scotch-cart tyre deflating. Sweat was running down his face making little rivulets through the dust that covered it.

I moved nearer to the bus. Its shell was crackling from the heat of the fire that had gutted it. It was lying on its side and I was too short to look through its windows that now faced the sky. I went around it and peered through the broken back window. I could not go very near because of the heat that was radiating from it. The interior of the bus was charred and smoke-filled. I looked closely. It seemed empty, with no signs of the remains of people or luggage. I remembered that I'd not heard anyone screaming.

Suddenly, Uncle Ndoro put his hand to his skull. He screamed as if he felt a sudden unbearable pain. I watched him helplessly as he took off at high speed up the big Saphela road in the direction of Godlwayo Secondary. At first I wanted to run with him, thinking that maybe something terrible was approaching us, maybe the soldiers again, but I saw nothing approaching, so I didn't move.

I watched Uncle Ndoro until he became a dark speck on the horizon and then suddenly he disappeared, and I knew that he had run down into a dip in the road.

I looked inside the bus again through the back window, almost as if expecting people to come tumbling out of it, people with burned bodies and peeling flesh. Then I remembered that when we'd seen the bus racing towards us, its roof carrier had been bare of luggage, meaning that maybe it was also empty of passengers as people travel with a lot of luggage when they're coming to the villages. I wondered why it had been racing – so much had happened since then – now the only answer that came to me was that perhaps it had been escaping the army truck that had appeared so soon afterwards. I wondered if the soldiers had also shown Uncle Ndoro the Headman's dead hand and threatened to cut off his, which would explain why he had been running away.

'Rudo!' A loud cry burst from behind me.

It was my mother! As I looked at her, her limbs seemed to wobble, and she fell to the ground like a log and lay still.

Chapter 5

Mother is a big woman, even bigger than father. Mother sometimes jokes that it's good that I have a small body, because two big women in the house would've been just too much for father. I've always hoped that mother would have another baby so that I could have somebody to play with at home as I like playing with babies, just as I do with Gift, Sithabile's little brother. This year mother nearly had another child, but when she came back from the clinic a month ago, she'd lost it. Her breasts are still producing milk, and she sometimes squeezes it out of them and throws it away.

When I saw mother fall to the ground, I nearly fell down as well. It was as if my world had collapsed. I just couldn't understand what was happening. I expected to wake up from a nightmare and find myself in bed at home.

I felt a little sob escape my lips. I quickly ran to mother and knelt beside her, and then I received another shock. There were dried tear-stains on her cheeks; she'd been crying. I have never seen mother cry. Even when she came from the clinic without the baby, she did not cry although her face looked very sad. Maybe she had cried at the clinic, but I had not seen tears on her face. Another bigger sob escaped me. Mother's face was so still it was as if she were dead.

Then I found myself crying and shaking mother's shoulders trying to wake her up. She had been wearing a brown wool hat and I had taken it off. A voice around me was also screaming, 'Mama, Mama, wake up, Mama!' Still crying, I threw my body over her. Then her arms went around me and I found myself held in a very tight grip. Mother's body heaved, and she sat up, her arms still tight around me. And then we were both sobbing and hugging each other. I love my mother, and I cannot imagine living without her. I love father too, but since he lives in the city I'm closer to mother.

I suddenly felt a presence and looked up. Uncle Ndoro was back. He was standing a little distance from us, and staring at the bus in concentration, almost as if he was trying to make out what it was. He seemed somehow shrunken, not the exuberant figure I knew so well. And then he howled and took off again at great speed in the direction of my home. I felt mother's body stiffen with anxiety.

'What's frightened him?' Mother's eyes darted around, searching up and down the road, and in the bushes around us. 'I don't see anything.'

'This is the second time he has done that,' I told her.

Mother was silent for a moment, digesting what I'd just told her. Then I felt her body relax a little, and she sighed heavily. Letting go of me, she heaved herself up onto her feet. 'Where did the soldiers go?' she asked, quickly taking her hat from my hand and putting it on again. Mother's hair is plaited but she wears her hat over the plaits to keep them clean; she only takes it off when we go to church on Sundays.

I pointed in the direction of Godlwayo village.

'Did you see your father?' Her voice was almost a whisper.

I shook my head, puzzled. Horror was building inside me again as I thought of the charred interior of the bus. Maybe everyone inside it had burned to ashes. 'Was he in the bus?'

'No, the bus was empty.' She was silent for a moment, her eyes fixed on her feet. 'Your father was the only passenger but he got off at home, then the soldiers captured him and drove off with him.' The words rushed out of her.

Then it struck me. The man with the sack on his head, the man whom I'd seen lying in the back of the army truck, whose figure looked familiar, was my father.

'I saw a man with his head covered in a sack in the back of the army

16

truck,' I whispered, desperately hoping that my mother would tell me that it wasn't him.

Mother sniffled. 'That was your father.' She fell silent again. I could see that she was preparing to say something else, something too heavy for her heart. She sniffled again and went on, 'The soldiers locked both your two uncles and their families in their homes and then burned down all the huts before the bus came.' She wiped her eyes with the back of her hand. 'And then they came to our home but when they heard me speak in Shona, they told me to run away. But I hid in the bushes, waiting for your father because I knew he would come in the bus...' her voice seemed to fade away. 'And then the bus came and when he got off it, the solders reappeared out of the bushes and captured him – only God knows if he's still alive now.' She started weeping.

'Did father commit a crime?'

'No. The soldiers said they're just killing all the Ndebele people, *maiwee zvangu!* What are people like us, who are married to Ndebele husbands, going to do?'

Tears started trickling down my cheeks. 'What are we going to do, mother?' All I could do was echo her words.

'I don't know, Rudo. I just don't know. But for now I have to make sure you're safe. As soon as the soldiers drove away with your father, I walked down the road, hoping I would meet you coming from school, and I'm glad I found you unharmed. But why are you alone?'

I told her what had happened to the other girls when we had met with the soldiers, and that I hoped the soldiers had released them when they had driven away because their clothes were no more there; I hoped they'd gone to their homes without my seeing them because I'd been hiding.

'I didn't meet them when I was coming this way,' mother said. 'Come my child, we have to hide. The devil has come to our village.'

And she led me off the road into the bush.

Chapter 6

Mbongolo village lies on the southern part of Saphela area, which is in the southern part of Kezi District. Far to the east, lining the horizon, are the towering peaks of the Phezulu mountains, and beyond them Plumtree District. If you walk in a southerly direction, you will finally come to the Botswana border. If you walk north you will reach Bulawayo.

As we walked through the bush and away from the crashed bus, I realised that mother was not going towards our home to the south, but walking east.

'Where are we going?' I asked as we cut across the bush.

Mother stopped walking, silent for a moment. Then two hares jumped out of a clump of bushes and I jumped back alarmed at the sudden noise.

'I don't know where we're going,' mother said at last. I felt a hollow sense of anxiety at the pit of my stomach. If mother – the one person I could trust in the world besides father – didn't know what to do, what would happen to us?

'Where's Auntie?' I asked. Auntie MaJamela, whom we simply call Auntie as if it's her first name, is the youngest in my father's family and she lives with us. How could I have forgotten her? All the terrible things that had happened had pushed her out of my mind. Uncle Genesis is the eldest, followed by Uncle Francis, then my father, and then Auntie. Uncle Genesis is Sithabile's father. But mother had just told me my uncles were now both dead, I prayed Auntie was not also dead.

'She left home early this morning to go to the clinic.' Auntie had been complaining of a headache, which mother had blamed on too much drinking, as over the last week Auntie had gone to Belinda's home for beer every evening. 'When the soldiers arrived, she had not yet returned. I hope she's still alive.' Mother echoed my prayer.

'Let's go home, Mother,' I gently pulled her hand in the direction of home, towards the south, and I was not surprised when she silently followed me.

I was now walking in front, but we were not following any path, just cutting through the bush. The sun was setting to our left, a large red fireball, almost the same colour as the soldier's red berets. I knew that if we walked fast, we would reach home before it was quite dark. Home represented security. And maybe we would find father there; maybe the soldiers had got what they wanted from him and had released him. I didn't dare think they had taken him because they wanted to cut off his hands to scare other school children, just as they had done to us with Chief Mabhena's hand.

***

We did not immediately go inside the yard on our return. Mother said we should hide behind the goat pen first, to see if it was safe to do so. Our animal pens are all at the back of our homestead. There are two: one for cattle, one for goats. We have four cows and six goats. Both pens were empty as in spring all the animals are let into the fields to feed on the dry stalks of the previous year's crops.

We stood for a while behind the goat pen. Our home has four huts: the kitchen, the main bedroom, the spare bedroom, which I share with Auntie whenever father is home, and the granary just behind the kitchen, which stands on tall stilts. The only movement around the huts was that of chickens and their chicks, which were pecking around the yard.

Finally, mother said it was safe.

'But let's not use the gates,' she said. We have two gates, a big one at the front, and a small one at the back, and we avoided them by squeezing through the wooden fence just behind the granary.

We crossed the yard and headed for the main bedroom. Then I saw Gadi, our dog. He was lying on his side by the kitchen hut; his legs were stretched out stiffly, almost as if he was a statue that had been toppled over. He's the only dog we have, and he's big and takes no nonsense from anybody. I walked over to him. His eyes were open. Flies buzzed around them. His body was perforated with holes that oozed blood, and were infested with more flies. I flinched and tears swarmed my eyes.

'They shot him when he tried to bite them when they were beating your father.' Mother's voice was flat. She was spreading soil with her foot over a large dark stain on the ground.

'What's that, Mama?'

She sniffed. 'Your father's blood; this is where they tortured him. I was hiding over there in the bushes after they'd told me to run away. They were beating him with a stick. His clothes were covered in blood; they kept shouting that he was a dead man. I can't tell you what else they did to him but finally their leader said they must take him away with them because they needed strong men to dig graves. I could've stayed with him and let them take me too, but then I thought of you.' Her voice trailed away.

After what felt like hours, I heard my voice asking, 'What are we going to do, Mama?' My voice sounded small, as if I was speaking from a long way away.

'I don't know,' mother replied, and then she added in a soft voice, 'I'm scared, my child, I can't lie to you about that.'

Then, her body tensed and she became still. I heard it too. It was the sound of an approaching vehicle, a heavy sound, like that of the army truck. Never again would I think it was a tractor.

Chapter 7

The sound of a car in the village has always been one that makes people – adults and children – stop whatever they're doing and watch the road, as if a good spirit is about to appear. It's a sound that contains a nostalgic reminder that we are a people filled with hope, and are not alone in the world.

But today was different. Mother grabbed my hand and we ran into the bedroom where she quickly shut and locked the door. Seeming to have recovered from her stupor, I recognised her familiar determination. In an instant, she had become the person I remembered, one who was firm in her decisions and reassuring to be with.

'Let's push the wardrobe against the door,' she said.

It was a heavy piece of furniture, but we managed to shove it across the room and against the door.

'Now, we must hide under the bed,' she said, and we crawled beneath it. Then she pulled the blanket down so that we couldn't be seen. Darkness enfolded us. The steady frightening roar of the truck sounded as if it was right outside our hut. Mother's protective arms were around me. We lay there quite still and silent listening intently to the sound of the engine, which slowly died away. Silence descended on the hut once again.

Outside I could hear the sound of the chickens. Under the bed, there was no light, and we lost all sense of time.

***

Eventually, I fell asleep. I had a dream. A soldier was carrying a long spliced stick in which dead hands and fingers were wriggling like worms, making all kinds of shapes; the biggest hand, with a ring in the shape of a cow with red eyes, beckoned me to draw nearer; then all the hands and fingers were crooked at me; all beckoning me to join them; then, suddenly, the hands became mice and they jumped off the stick and clambered over the soldier, who tried to beat them off as one would beat off flies; then the mice became Sithabile and the other girls who'd disappeared after I'd left them with the soldiers, and they were all screaming one long-drawn-out scream.

I woke with a start. My heart was beating hard and fast. Mother's arms were still tight around me and I could smell her comforting scent of wood smoke and sweat. The scream in my dream was still there; it had become a long-drawn-out wail; it was a person grieving. It was a woman. Mother's grip grew tighter, but it was not she who was wailing. Faint and far away, we could hear other wails, which seemed like the echoes of the louder wail, which seemed right outside our hut.

'It's Auntie,' mother said her voice breaking. '*Mwari wangu*, what's happening to us!' Mother speaks fluent Ndebele, but when she's tormented she uses Shona.

We remained frozen together under the bed. The wail outside continued, one long pitiful sound after another, whilst the others far off haunted the night like lost and wounded creatures.

Then mother released me from her embrace, the movement sharp. 'No,' she said. 'This can't go on, we're all going to become mad.'

She eased herself out from underneath the bed, and I followed her. The room was in darkness, but a moonbeam coming through the small window gave a little light. Mother, crouching, moved to the window, the shape of her head outlined by the moon outside. I was standing behind her.

My parent's bedroom has a sharp smell of mothballs, which are placed in the wardrobe to protect our clothes from termites. Maybe it was the darkness or the sense of doom that pervaded the room, but the acrid minty smell seemed very intense.

Suddenly, mother began pushing at the wardrobe with her back and

I moved to help her. The wail outside was maddening. The wardrobe screeched across the floor as we moved it away from the door. Mother unlocked the door and we glided quietly outside.

A full moon sat in the sky, like a thoughtful eye. The yard was revealed by the moonlight, clear and sharp. The wailing still hung around the village, like a choir of witches. There was no one in our yard. Then mother headed for the front gate, and I followed close behind her.

In front of our home is a small hillock. At that moment, it seemed like a finger raised in warning. This hillock hides our home from Saphela road. We walked around it. Beyond lie the homes of Uncle Genesis and Uncle Francis. I was walking in trepidation. I remembered mother telling me earlier that my two uncles and their families had all been killed. But I couldn't imagine them dead. I had never seen a dead person though I have attended wakes and never liked the atmosphere.

Uncle Genesis's home is on our side of the road, and that of Uncle Francis's is on the other side. As we rounded the hillock, we heard the wailing voice, which we had thought was in our yard. When we reached the gate of Uncle Genesis's homestead, all we could see were five round shadows indicating where the huts of the homestead had once been.

A figure, lit by moonlight, was kneeling before one of the dark shadows. It was wailing. I felt a cold shiver run through me.

Mother moved towards this figure, with me following close behind. A strange smell of roasted meat filled the air, but all our attention was on this one living figure. We stepped over the bodies of three dead dogs: Skelemu, Danger, and Basop, all belonging to Uncle Genesis. One couldn't approach Uncle Genesis's home without the dogs barking, even if they knew you, and Skelemu had been the most dangerous of them all, just like our Gadi. They would never bark again.

We reached the kneeling figure and mother stopped. Then the wail became a voice.

'Oh Genesis, my brother, Oh Genesis, my brother!' It was Auntie. As I recognised her, I also saw in the middle of the charred floor a dark mound, like burned sacks piled one on top of the other.

'They're all dead. Even Francis and his family,' Auntie wailed. 'What did they ever do to anybody? And to die like this? Burned alive! Ooooooh,' her voice broke with the weight of grief. '*Nkulunkulu wami.* That owl, the one hooting outside our home, was an omen.'

Auntie had tried several times to throw stones at the owl hooting in the *mopane* tree at our front gate. It would fly away and then after a while it would return, and at night we would hear it hooting again.

Mother put her hand on Auntie's shoulder.

'There's nothing we can do now,' I heard mother say softly. 'They've gone to join our ancestors.'

'Genesis and Francis never did anything to anybody. Never...' Auntie wailed, but her voice wasn't so loud. 'They were not dissidents, just simple people looking after their families and their livestock.'

Still kneeling, she pressed her face into mother's skirt and mother placed her hands on Auntie's shoulders, and with the human contact came a fresh outburst of sobs.

Mother did not say anything. The wailing from the village hung in the air. I felt a big lump rise in my throat.

Chapter 8

Mother and Auntie are always arguing, especially when Auntie is drunk.
I think, sometimes, that they don't like each other. When Auntie is
drunk she often assumes a superior attitude and says mother and I are
rat-eating people. Mother never argues but just tells her quietly that
Shona people do not eat rats, only mice, and they are delicious.

I remember one day when I was at primary school, father had
caught a mouse in a trap in our maize field and mother had roasted it
on a fire. We'd eaten the small rodent, all three of us sharing it, and it
had tasted just like roast chicken. I'd asked father if we couldn't catch
more mice and have them for supper at home, and father had laughed
and said, 'Do you want Auntie to call us rat-eaters?'

I sometimes dream of walking with my mother across a valley of tall
dry grass together with an old man carrying a long spliced stick with
rows of mice on it. One day I told mother my dream and she said it
wasn't a dream but that it had happened in Chisara when I was a child,
and when she used to accompany her father hunting for mice. She said
that the man in the dream was grandfather Mamvura, who has since
died. I was born in Chisara. Mother says we joined father in Mbongolo
village when I was three, and he had paid lobola for her.

Auntie was pressing her face in mother's skirt, seeking comfort,
and mother had her hands on Auntie's shoulder, giving it. Then
I cocked my ears thinking I could hear the faint sound of a child
crying. I quickly shut the idea out of my mind, thinking it was a trick

of my imagination.

'The soldiers came to the clinic and burned it down too,' Auntie said in a muffled voice. 'I had just left, so I quickly hid in the bushes. They ordered the nurses to undress and they took them all away, naked, just like that.'

'So much has happened today,' mother said gently. 'Try to put it out of your mind for now, Auntie.'

Auntie's shoulders heaved as another terrible sob escaped from her.

Then I heard the faint cry of the baby again. I saw mother's hands freeze on Auntie's back.

'Did you hear that?'

'Hear what?' Auntie asked, and a hyena laughed, as if in answer. 'You mean the hyena?' Another hyena laugh followed the first one.

'No,' mother replied. 'I thought I heard the sound of a child crying.'

'I heard it too,' I said. 'I thought I was imagining it.'

Then we all stood silent. The wails from the village rang through the darkness, as if they had always been there, like the moon and the stars, as if the whole world was wailing. We stood listening for the cry of the child. The moonlight fell on Auntie's face and the streaks of tears on her cheeks shone with a pale blue light.

Then we heard a sudden burst of gunfire. The sound was heart-stopping. Instinctively, I clung to mother. The gunfire seemed to be coming from all around us, but we didn't see a flash of bullets across the night sky. Then the gunfire died away and in the silence we realised that the wailing had stopped.

And then we heard the cry of the baby again, faint, as if from inside a house with no windows and a closed door. I felt myself shiver. I hoped it wasn't a ghost.

'I can hear the baby too,' Auntie said, standing up. There was a mortar and a pestle lying next to the ruins of the kitchen. Mother walked over and picked up the pestle, then she stepped over to the charred mound in the middle of the hut. The pestle was about her height, and as thick as her arm.

I wondered what she wanted to do. Then we heard cry of the baby again. This time, it was unmistakable, but it was hard for me to tell

26

where it was coming from. I saw mother push the pestle into the mound, then she tried to lever it up, but it was too heavy for her. Auntie moved to help her and the two women levered the pestle up, and the whole mound fell apart; I retched and bile filled my mouth.

What had seemed one thing was many, a mass of human bodies, burnt together: charred limbs, bones shining white in the moonlight, and defaced skulls. The stench of burnt flesh was intense. My stomach heaved and I quickly knelt down and vomited.

When I looked up through tear-blinded eyes, I saw that mother and Auntie were still attacking the mound. Each time they heaved the pestle up, the remains of more bodies toppled over to the side.

Uncle Genesis had had a family of six. At last only one body remained on the floor. It was not as burnt as the others had been. Its upper body was still intact, and I clearly saw the face. It was Auntie MaDube, Uncle Genesis's wife. She was lying on sheets of asbestos. I remembered these sheets. They had always stood against the wall inside Uncle Genesis's bedroom. Sithabile had told me that one day they would provide the roof of the five-roomed modern house that her father was planning to build in his homestead one day.

The child's cry seemed louder, and it seemed to be coming from underneath MaDube's body. Then I saw mother and Auntie lift the asbestos sheet with MaDube's body on it and lay it to one side. After that they lifted each of the sheets off the floor, one by one, and each time they did so, we could hear the baby's cry more clearly.

There were ten sheets. The last two had shattered, so mother and Auntie just shoved the pieces to one side, and right in the middle of the floor was a metal handle. Mother and Auntie both pulled at the handle and through the grime I saw a trapdoor rise to reveal a hole on the floor. And from inside the hole rose a blast of fresh screaming, the sound of a frightened, angry, hungry baby.

I knew about this hole. Mother and Auntie must have known about it too, although we never talked about it. Uncle Genesis had it dug in his bedroom, so that he could use it as a safe for important things, and to hide money from thieves and dissidents, Sithabile had told me. Normally, a small table was placed over the trapdoor handle, but it must have burnt together with everything else in the house.

Mother reached down into the hole. Auntie and I watched spellbound as she lifted a baby out of the darkness.

It was screaming. Mother placed it gently against her shoulder and shushed at it, and then she stepped back towards Auntie. I rose unsteadily to my feet and wiped the tears from my eyes with my hand. We stared at the baby in wonderment. It was Gift, Uncle Genesis's last-born child. He was five months old. And he was dressed in cream wool jumpers with a matching hat on his little head.

'*Mwari wangu,*' mother said, inspecting the baby. 'He seems not to be burnt. His clothes are wet but not burnt. Surely, if he was hurt, he would not stop crying, but he has.'

Mother removed her breast from her blouse and Gift immediately started suckling hungrily.

'Whoever put the child inside that hole made the right decision,' mother said, 'Now it's our duty to see that this baby lives, Auntie, and also Rudo here.'

'They're the only ones of all our children now left,' Auntie said. 'They must live.' I nearly mentioned Sithabile, as I thought she might still be alive, but the words failed to come out of my mouth.

With the baby still suckling, mother went down on her knees, and asked us also to do the same.

The moon still sat in the sky, as if worried about what was happening to us. The night was silent. There was not even a breath of a wind, or trill of crickets.

'*Mwari wedu,*' mother started praying. 'We thank you **Mwari wedu** for keeping your little baby alive in the middle of a fire, and without your kindness this would never have happened. We thank you **Mwari wedu** for being our father when we are in need, and we ask that you show us the way to safety so that our children can live and grow up to be adults also. We also pray to you **Mwari wedu** to look after all the dead and raise your hand against all those who have sinned against you today. We ask for protection in this dangerous time, **Mwari wedu**, in the name of the son and the Holy Spirit. Amen.'

Chapter 9

After we had returned home, Mother began preparing a meal of
isitshwala and *ulude* on the fire in the kitchen. The door was closed
tight so that light from the fire could not be seen, and we had draped
a cloth over the window. Auntie sat listlessly beside me on a reed mat.
I was holding Gift, who was wrapped in an old white baby dress and
a yellow shawl mother had taken from a bag in the bedroom where all
my old clothes are kept. 'I don't know what we can do now,' mother
said as she stirred the mealie-meal, her worried face lit by the fire.

'We have to find out what is happening,' Auntie said. 'It's difficult to
sit like this in the darkness.'

'And how can we find out, Auntie? You heard the wailing, and also
the gunfire.'

'But we must know, Mamvura,' repeated Auntie. 'It's so frightening
just sitting here, not knowing what's happening around us. Let's go to
the Headman, he's the person who will know.'

'I don't think the Headman is still alive,' mother said, and she told
Auntie my story about how the soldiers had come upon us girls at the
site of the bus crash, and how they terrified us with the dead hand of
Headman Mabhena.

'So you see,' said mother, 'most probably he was also burnt alive in
his home with his family.'

It felt strange sitting there, waiting for our supper, talking about
the day's events, almost as if they had happened to someone else at

another far-off time. I was exhausted and I wanted to put my head down and cry and cry, but instead I was nursing Gift, and his little body comforted me somehow.

'What about Sithabile and the other girls?' Auntie asked. 'Does anyone know where they are now?'

'Rudo was separated from her friends when the soldiers chased her away, so it's anybody's guess, but what I know is that Sithabile was not there when the soldiers came to Uncle Genesis's home.'

'So she might still be alive somewhere,' Auntie said. 'Then why doesn't she come here to us?'

'Maybe she can't come right now,' mother said. 'Let's just pray that she's still alive wherever she is and we will find her one day, if we all live through this.'

Auntie just shook her head. Then a jackal laughed outside, and several others answered with more laughter.

'Do you think we should bury them?' Auntie pointed in the direction of Uncle Genesis's homestead. 'Otherwise the jackals will eat their bones and that's not right. Our ancestors won't accept such a terrible thing.'

'Maybe we should,' mother said. 'But will we manage on our own? There are too many bodies – and you know, Auntie, we're all scared to be out there alone.'

Auntie fell silent. The jackal laughed again, and the other jackals laughed in response. It was chilling, as we all knew what they intended to do, and there was nothing we could do to stop them.

'Mother,' I said. 'Why don't we switch on the radio?' We have a small set that is kept in the bedroom. 'Maybe there will be something about this on the news.' Part of me just wanted to shift our attention away from the jackals.

Mother dished food onto two plates: one for the *isitshwala*, and the other for *ulude*.

'You're right, Rudo,' mother said. 'Why didn't I think of that? Auntie, please go and fetch the radio for us.'

Mother put a dish of water down for us to wash our hands. The fire had sunk to embers, which provided the only light in the room, and the shadows played eerily on the walls. We waited for Auntie to come back.

***

We have been living with Auntie for about two years. Before then she had had a home in Dabulani village, which is the fourth village after Godlwayo, Mbongolo, and Lotshe in the Saphela area. She was married to a man called Sibanda, long before mother and I came to live with father in Mbongolo.

Auntie and Sibanda had not had any children. Whenever Auntie has drunk beer, and if father is home from the city, she likes to discuss the break-up of her marriage with him. She always concludes by asking if what her husband did was fair. Auntie says that she left Sibanda because, after nine years, she had not given him children, and he had married a second wife, openly declaring that he wanted children with her, ones that Auntie could not give him. The second wife had immediately given birth to triplets. After that, Sibanda started mistreating Auntie, often beating her up, until finally she left.

The door opened and Auntie came back with the radio, a black Supersonic transistor, the size of a small brick.

'Switch it on please,' mother said. 'We will listen as we eat.'

The radio is always set to Radio Two, which is our favourite station as it's in the vernacular. I didn't know what the time was, but it must have been very late. English music was playing on the radio. Mother asked Auntie to set the volume very low, so that the sound did not carry, and I placed the sleeping Gift on the mat, and we washed our hands and started eating.

We did not talk as we ate. I suddenly found I was very hungry. Even as we ate, our concentration was on the radio, which was balanced against the wall. I was willing the music to stop and the radio to explain the nightmare unravelling around us.

Finally, the English song ended, and a male voice announced the time: 10:15 p.m. It was followed by a progamme in Ndebele on agriculture.

'The news will come at eleven,' mother said.

After we'd finished eating, Auntie washed the plates and pots and put them away in the mud cupboard on the wall.

Gift was still asleep, although now and then he would give a tiny snort. I wondered how long he had been buried under the asbestos sheets while his family burned above him.

'Do you think the war has come back?' Auntie asked. We were all sitting staring at the glowing embers.

'Between who and who?' mother asked.

Auntie was silent for a moment. 'Now, between us black people.'

'It's impossible,' mother replied. 'I don't think something like that can happen in this country so soon after independence.'

'But we've seen the dissidents, Mamvura, and they say they're fighting the government,' Auntie said. 'Maybe there's now a full-scale war between the dissidents and the soldiers.'

I've also seen the dissidents several times in the village, but I've never really understood what they want. Mother says that the dissidents are guerrillas who refused to give up their guns after independence. But are they fighting the government, like Auntie says, because one day last year, they robbed Uncle Genesis's store. Sithabile and I had been playing on the veranda when two men appeared out of the bush. They were both carrying guns and looked unkempt; their clothes were torn and dirty. It was late and there were no customers around, just Sithabile's mother, MaDube, who kept shop. The men went into the store, we heard loud voices and a moment later they ran out and disappeared among the trees. A moment later, MaDube came out looking shocked. She had been robbed of the day's takings and two loaves of bread.

How can people fight the government by robbing our stores? It makes no sense to me.

I've also noticed that people talk very carefully about the dissidents. I guess they're afraid of them, because a few months ago they shot a man dead in Belinda's home during a beer drink. Auntie witnessed it, and told us that the dissidents had said the man was a 'government sell-out'.

'It's hard to believe the people today were really government soldiers,' mother continued. 'Government soldiers are trained and disciplined, and they wouldn't go around burning up people and children in their homes.'

The jackal laughed outside again, and its friends laughed with it.

Chapter 10

Mother was given our radio last year by Uncle Ndoro. He's always selling things when he comes to the village, especially second-hand clothes, cooking oil, sugar, and transistor radios. Sometimes, in the rainy season, he asks mother to trade his goods for bags of *mopane* worms; last year she did good business for him, which is why he gave her the radio. Mother says that Uncle Ndoro sells the caterpillars in Chisara. People there like them very much as they are nutritious and nice to eat when they're cooked properly.

The radio was an instant success in our home. Our favourite programme has always been the drama, Sakhelene Zinini, which plays in the early evening on Mondays and Thursdays, and we always listen to it as a family.

But tonight felt very different. We were anxious and afraid, and we were playing the radio very quietly, waiting for the news to come on. Finally, we heard the familiar roll of drums that comes before the news. The news is always read first in Shona, then in Ndebele, and lastly in English.

Auntie doesn't speak or understand Shona and so she was watching mother and I attentively. The newsreader, a woman, first began with the news that the Prime Minister was on a state visit to the United Kingdom, where he was going to be given an honorary degree by the University of Edinburgh. She then went on to report that the O-level results had been better this year than last, and that we were well on our way to having the highest literacy rate in Africa. More news followed about an invasion of locusts in Matabeleland North, and new government houses being built in Gwelo. Finally, the Zimbabwean national soccer team was going to play Zambia in a friendly match, and then the news in Shona ended. There was a roll of drums and an advertisement for Coca-Cola.

Mother was incredulous. 'Nothing!' Astonishment was written all over her face.

'Nothing?' Auntie asked. 'Did you hear correctly, Mamvura?'

'Absolutely nothing,' mother said, 'though they mentioned that the Prime Minister is out of the country.'

'Maybe they missed it and will say something about it in Ndebele,' Auntie said hopefully. Then she raised her hand for silence as we heard the drum roll preceding the news in Ndebele. Our ears pricked up, but it was an exact repeat of the news in Shona, except that afterwards there was an advertisement for Colgate toothpaste.

'Maybe the soldiers have gone wild because the Prime Minister is not here,' Auntie said. 'Somebody should report them to the police. They're going to rot in jail for this. We have very tough laws in Zimbabwe, as if they didn't know.'

Mother was silent, seeming to be deep in thought. The English version of the news was now being read and again we stopped to listen to it, though Mother and Auntie don't understand English. I can understand a little bit, but not when it becomes deep. However, I understood enough to know it was just a repetition of the Shona and Ndebele versions. Then an Ndebele programme began: the announcer was reading letters from people with health problems and giving them advice.

'We should go to the primary school,' Auntie said, switching off the radio. 'There's a telephone there and the headmaster can phone the police and report what's happening.' The nearest police station is at Maphisa Growth Point, which is very far away towards Bulawayo City.

'That's a good idea,' mother said. 'But should we do that now or in the morning?'

'Let's do it now,' Auntie said. 'The soldiers might come back.'

'But I'll go to the school alone,' mother said. I felt my heart lurch. 'You stay here with the children, Auntie, we can't risk taking them with us at this time of night. And, since I speak Shona, I've a better chance of getting safely to the school and back.'

'Yes, that's a good idea,' Auntie replied, 'but what if the soldiers return whilst you're away?'

'I'm frightened like you, Auntie. I fear for all of us, and for Rudo's father. Where is he? What's happening to him? Why did they choose to keep him alive? Do they have a worse fate for him than they had for those they killed immediately?' She took a deep breath to control her voice, which had begun to wobble.

'I don't believe they're government soldiers,' said Auntie suddenly. 'They're some devil force that needs to be reported to the police and caught before they can do any further damage.'

'Let me go to the primary school,' mother said, standing up.

'Do you want us to stay in the kitchen?' Auntie asked.

'I'm also afraid to stay here,' I said. 'We can hide in the bush until you come back, Mother.' For the first time, the open bush represented more security than the solid confines of the hut, where it would be easy for someone to trap us inside.

'You can hide behind the goat pen,' mother said. 'No one can see you there if they come from the road. Take some blankets with you.'

'Please watch out for Sithabile,' Auntie said. 'The poor girl might be lost somewhere out there.'

***

We took two blankets from the bedroom and went out through the gate at the back. Mother was still with us as we prepared to hide. She was carrying Gift, who was still asleep. Auntie and I laid one blanket on the ground behind the goat pen, sat down and pulled the other one over our feet. Mother placed Gift between us, and then she disappeared into the moonlit night, headed in the direction of the primary school on a small path that would keep her hidden from the main road.

I blinked back tears as I watched her leave. I didn't want her to go, I wanted her to stay with us.

Chapter 11

The scent of goat dung was overwhelming but that was the least of our worries. Auntie said we must lie back and pull the blanket over us, and we did so. We didn't talk much. Auntie only talks a lot when she's drunk beer: that's when she turns nasty and reveals another side of her character.

Although Auntie has a nasty side, she's a hard worker. We share our maize field with her, and there she even outworks mother, often remaining alone in the field long after we've returned home. Even in the homestead, she is never still, and our yard is one of the cleanest in the village. Mother always says that Auntie takes after Uncle Francis, a very strong and hard-working man.

***

Uncle Francis was the second born in my father's family. First there was Uncle Genesis; my father and Auntie MaJamela come after Uncle Francis. With two wives and eight children, Uncle Francis farmed a field bigger than all the others in our village; so, in a good year, he harvested the most and often sold maize to other villagers who had not met with such good fortune. He was a strong man who often went around without a shirt. Some villagers said that he smoked mbanje, claiming that this was why he farmed such a big field from sunrise to sunset with few small breaks. Even in times of drought Uncle Francis managed to harvest, as he'd dug a very deep well in his field; he helped my father and Uncle Genesis to dig wells in their fields, too, though they soon dried up.

Occasionally, Uncle Francis would take his maize to the city to sell, and when he came back he would bring bottles of spirits and invite other villagers to come for a party in his homestead and play records on his briefcase gramophone for the whole night. Sometimes I would go to Uncle's Francis's home when he was playing records, to play with my cousins and dance with the adults.

I remember when I used to visit Uncle's Francis's home as a child, he would scoop me up in his huge arms and swing me in the air, joking, 'I'm going to throw you so high you will land in Chisara and see how your grandparents are doing over there.'

And now, even Uncle Francis with his strong body is lost to us.

***

Auntie had her head under the blanket and kept Gift snug in the crook of her arm, but I kept my head out. I don't like sleeping with my head under a blanket, unless it is a really cold, and tonight I wanted to see what was happening around us.

All my senses were on the alert. I could hear the usual trill of crickets and little animals rustling in the undergrowth. The moon was directly overhead. I found myself wishing that it was a mirror that would reflect back to us the image of mother on her way to the primary school, so that we could see if she was safe.

In any other circumstances, it would have been a beautiful night. The stars that were furthest from the moon were the brightest; as if the further away they were, the more confident they were of their light.

I've never slept the whole night outside, but there are times, especially on warm evenings, when we sit around a fire in our yard until late into the evening. On such nights, I like to lie on the ground and gaze at the sky, often forming dreams around the stars. I feel the shooting stars are ideas that have become excited and want to land somewhere on earth to become real ideas in people's minds and bring light and excitement to life.

Then Gift stirred and woke up. He started babbling happily, as if he was talking to somebody only seen by him. It was hard to believe that just a few hours ago he'd been right in the middle of a furnace that had incinerated his entire family. I shifted and put my hand on his little body and shushed him, but instead his voice rose. Auntie woke up and she tried shushing him too. But the more we tried, the happier he became and the more noise he made. Then I offered him my thumb and he began sucking on it with small nuzzling sounds.

I wanted to sleep but I couldn't. My mind continued to race, playing over and again the events of the day. After a while, I heard Auntie groaning and I reached across the baby and touched her. She was shivering, as if she was cold.

'What's the matter?' I felt a sudden panic. Auntie did not reply immediately, and when she did, her voice was so low it was almost inaudible.

'I'm very cold,' she said. 'I think I'm ill. The cold is inside my bones, but I feel hot as well; touch my forehead and see for yourself.'

'Yes it's hot,' I said. 'What's the matter?'

'I don't know.'

I was at a loss. I didn't know what to say or do as mother would have done and a heavy silence fell between us. I took Gift's little hand in mine and was somehow comforted to feel him clutch my fingers.

Then through the earth I picked up the vibrations of a vehicle. I looked towards Auntie, but she was lying with her face to the sky. Auntie has good looks, but she's more handsome than pretty, and she has a few little hairs on her chin. From the set of her head, I knew she had not felt the vibrations. I raised my head a little and the sound disappeared. I placed my head back on the ground once more, and again I heard a faint growl. I felt my body go rigid and my heart start beating hard. My fingers tightened and Gift gave a loud excited cry. I immediately put my hand over his mouth to quieten him, but he struggled, and I took it away, fearful that he would cry out again.

'Auntie?'

'I can hear it. It's coming this way.' Then in one swift movement, she stood up and peered over the fence of the goat pen. I remained on the ground, holding Gift close to me.

'What can you see?' I asked. My thoughts had leapt to mother. Where was she? I hoped the soldiers had not found her after they'd given her a warning to run away. If they caught her again, they would surely not make things easy for her.

Auntie seemed to have recovered. Her body was taut as she crouched shoulder height at the fence.

'I can't see anything yet,' she whispered. 'This isn't good, Rudo. Do you think we should follow your mother?'

'If we try to follow her, we might miss her.' I didn't want to lose mother and she'd told us that she would come back to the homestead, so I didn't want to leave.

Then Auntie ducked.

'There are three cars,' she whispered.

More soldiers? I expected Auntie to make a decision about what we should do – stay or run away. If these vehicles were filled with soldiers who decided to search any of the homes that had not been burnt down that afternoon, we might be discovered. What if they decided to kill us, just as they had killed our dog?

The sound of the engines grew louder. Their headlights probed the night around us. Auntie said we must hide under the blanket again. We lay flat and pulled the top blanket over our heads, but Gift cried out sharply and tried to pull the blanket off. Making soothing sounds, Auntie held him close and he stopped crying. The sound grew louder by the moment. I had a feeling that the vehicles would leave the road, plough through our home and the goat pen, and then continue on their journey as if nothing had happened. We lay as still as stone, and Gift seemed to feel the atmosphere and kept very quiet. Then the roar of heavy trucks was on top of us. I cringed under the blanket, wanting the earth to open up and hide us. Then the roar passed us and droned away until at last it disappeared. Shaking with relief, we came out from under the blanket and sat up.

Chapter 12

A little while later, a figure materialised out of the darkness, walking fast. It was mother. She was breathing heavily.

'We have to leave now!' Her voice was terse, and frightened.

'Did you get to the school?' Auntie asked.

'There's big trouble that way, the soldiers have camped at the primary school and three more trucks, also filled with soldiers, arrived just as I reached there.'

'We saw the trucks when they passed us,' Auntie interjected.

'I didn't go into the school,' mother continued. 'But I watched from a distance. They have made a jail with a fence of barbed wire in the middle of the football ground and put people inside it. Everyone is naked: men, women and children. It's horrible. Horrible. While I was watching, some people broke free and ran away. The soldiers' shot at them, several fell to the ground, but some managed to flee into the darkness. The soldiers are now hunting for them. They might come this way. We have to leave right now, go as far away as we can, and look for a place to hide. First, let's take a few things that we might need. Let's be quick.'

'But mother, what if father's escaped?' I asked. 'He might come home and we'll miss him.'

'I thought of that, Rudo. But I don't think he could've been amongst those who escaped. He would have reached here already. We mustn't waste time. Let's go.'

We raced to the bedroom hut. Then mother asked Auntie to stay outside with Gift and keep watch. I went into the room with her. All our clothes, even Auntie's, are kept in the wardrobe. Mother worked swiftly in the weak moonlight. 'We'll each take two dresses and jerseys,' mother said, as she threw garments onto the bed. 'We need some of your old baby clothes for Gift.' Then she took a big travelling bag from the top of the wardrobe, emptied its contents on the floor, and stuffed our clothes and two tightly folded blankets inside.

We came out of the hut, with mother carrying the bag. Auntie stood, a motionless figure, hugging the wall, a still silent Gift in her arms.

Mother placed the travelling bag at Auntie's feet. 'Let me get some things from the kitchen,' she said. Coals still glowed in the hearth. She took an empty plastic bag and filled it with food – *inkobe*, a bundle of lion biltong that she had bought from a hunter, and a ball of cabbage. She also put two plates and cups into the bag, a tablespoon, a knife, and a small pot.

'Those soldiers took away all the groceries your father had brought us from town,' mother said as she was filling the heavy plastic bag. She was speaking quickly. 'And also the present he promised you.' I'd forgotten about the present, and wondered how mother could think of it at such a difficult time.

Next, we filled an old cooking oil container with water. Then mother stood looking around the room, a slight frown on her forehead wondering if there was anything she'd forgotten.

At that moment, Auntie rushed into the room.

'There's a truck coming up the road from the primary school!' she whispered, fear choking her voice. The bag of clothes was already on her back, and Gift was clutched to her bosom.

'Let's go Rudo!' mother said. I grabbed the radio from the floor and we ran out of the room. Mother was carrying the water container and the bag of food.

From the yard, we could see headlights coming towards us from the direction of the primary school. We raced across the yard, through the gate at the back, past the animal pens, and into the bush.

'Run, Rudo,' mother panted. I was in front just searching for somewhere to hide.

***

A little distance into the bush, we stopped to catch our breath. We'd only just made it. The vehicle was turning onto the track that led to our home. It entered our gate and stopped, its headlights throwing the whole homestead into relief. Dark figures moved into the light in front of the car.

Soldiers. They were pushing a man before them. One of them kicked him hard on the back and he fell to the ground.

Mother gasped in shock. *'Mwari wangu!'*

I froze, my eyes on the slumped figure. It was father, and he was naked, the lights of the truck illuminating his body. Slowly, he sat up. I recognised the soldier with reading glasses. He was pointing something at father's head. I knew it was a pistol.

Suddenly mother took my head and buried it in her bosom. I did not struggle. I waited for the shot. In my heart I said goodbye to father. Images tumbled through my mind. He'd been a father who liked to laugh with his family, a man who was kind to other people, who had gone all the way to Chisara in Mashonaland East to pay lobola for his Shona bride and bring her back to his village in Matabeleland in triumph. A hard-working man who'd left the village to work in the city in the factories so that he could take care of us. I could not imagine a better man than that, or a life without him.

The moment seemed to stretch into eternity, time that would be brought to a stop by a single gunshot. Somehow I felt that when that came, it would also shoot through my head, and I would also die. Tears flowed from my eyes. I was weeping for my father, whom I considered already dead.

'They're not going to shoot him,' I heard Auntie say. 'They're not going to shoot him.' There was hope in her voice. Mother's eyes must have been closed too, because when Auntie spoke, her chin lifted sharply from my head.

I slowly turned round and looked towards home. Father was now standing. His back seemed bent, and his arms half raised in surrender, like a man who wants to give up on life, but is considering holding onto a rope that's hanging before him.

A soldier detached himself from the group. He went first to the main bedroom and kicked its door open – the sound of the kick reverberating through the air. He looked inside, and then he moved to the kitchen, peered inside, and then he went to the spare bedroom. The door crashed open. Satisfied there was nothing there, the soldier returned to the others standing impatiently at the truck and said something to the soldier in the reading glasses. It was frightening to think that they must have been looking for us, and if they had found us, what the soldiers would have done to us.

The soldiers' faces were lit by a sudden flare and one of them handed a flaming stick to father and then pushed him towards the bedroom hut.

Father staggered a bit, and then steadying himself, he stood still, the torch flaming in his hands.

'Dear lord God,' I heard Auntie say softly. 'Please no.'

I saw father turn around and face the soldiers. He seemed to be saying something to them as I saw his head move and his free hand gesture, but his voice did not reach us.

The soldier who had pushed father barked something at him in a loud voice, and the sound reached us: the words were not intelligible, but we did not need to be told what they meant. Then the soldier raised his rifle again and pointed it at father's head.

'Please do what they say,' I heard mother say in a soft, broken voice. 'Just do it. Your daughter is watching. We will build another home.'

I also willed father to obey mother's plea.

'Move, Innocent,' I heard Auntie whisper, calling father by his first name.

As if in answer to our prayers, father moved. He walked to the bedroom hut, but instead of torching the thatch roofing, he went inside the hut.

'No!' I heard myself crying out in a loud voice. Mother immediately clamped one hand over my mouth, whilst the other gripped me around my chest. I struggled, my eyes on the bedroom hut which now glowed from inside, but mother's hands were too strong. I wanted to run to the hut – but father suddenly came out of it, raised the flaming torch and touched it to the thatched roof, which instantly caught fire. He walked to the kitchen hut and disappeared inside. I relaxed, and mother released me.

Father then emerged from the kitchen, and also set its roof alight. By now the roof of the bedroom was blazing and the flames lit up our homestead and the army truck, which had been backed to the gate. We could now see all the soldiers, about fifteen of them, and they all had their eyes fixed on father. Father next set the spare bedroom roof alight, and, as if that was not enough, the soldiers also made him burn our granary. When the granary caught fire, I saw our chickens leap from the struts below it and disappear into the night.

Then, in the light of the flames, the soldiers got back into the truck, hustling father in with them.

The vehicle went out of the gate and headed back up the road in the direction of Mbongolo Primary School.

Chapter 13

Mother was now leading us. Gift was on her back, and she also held the water container. I followed close behind her with the plastic bag of food on my head; Auntie was behind me with the travelling bag on her back, into which she had put our radio.

Even though our home was now a long way behind us, I could still feel the flames; it was as if a part of me had also been burned away, something I would never again recover. My feet were heavy as we walked further and further away from the only place I knew as home. The heaviness was coming from my heart. Everything seemed so hopeless and I did not have the sense that we were going anywhere that would bring us comfort.

I'd expected that we would meet other people also fleeing the soldiers, but strangely the veld was empty of human life, except that some of the bushes seemed to assume human forms in the moonlight. I wondered where everyone was and if we'd been the only ones to escape. Maybe most people had been burned to death in their homes, or were now prisoners within the barbed wire fence at the primary school.

After what seemed like hours, the moon slid below the tree line to the north of us, and a deep darkness settled on the land. The stars, now that the moon was gone, seemed to shine even more brightly, as if a new fire had been lit inside them, lending an electric glow to the vast sky. I had never been awake so late but strangely was not tired, as if fear had switched on a light in my mind.

I was familiar with the area we were walking through on the outskirts of Mbongolo village. The part reserved for fields lay ahead. I suspected that mother was leading us to our field, but I did not ask.

I was proved right when we came to a path that I instantly recognised as the one that goes past Uncle Francis's big field; our field comes after his. It's not so big, but big enough to provide us with all the crops we need during a good season. It's about an hour's walk from home to our field, but we seemed not to have travelled that long. Mother led us to the gate.

The central point in our field is the **ingalani**, which we repair at the beginning of every harvest season to keep it strong for the crops that it will hold. Beside this towering wood structure is a **marula** tree. When we come to work in the field, its shade provides a good place to rest, or to leave the things that we had brought with us.

Mother led us to the **marula** tree and we came to a stop beneath it. I could see the hunched shadows of our cows, and hear the crunching of dry vegetation as they grazed. I couldn't see the goats. Auntie and I had driven the animals to the field last Saturday, and every day since then either mother or Auntie walked them to a dam about fifteen minutes away.

'We can rest here until sunrise,' mother said. 'We'll decide what to do in the morning – I don't think the soldiers will come this far as there are no homes in this area.' She unfastened the towel that held Gift on her back. Then, after she had cautioned us to be careful with the water, we all had a drink from the container.

We sat under the tree, but before we had even had time to feel our weariness, we jumped to our feet again. We could hear singing of a kind I'd never heard before, and it seemed to be coming our way. The voices were male. Mother was already tying Gift onto her back again.

'It's the soldiers! They're coming this way. I heard them singing that song at the primary school. They must be on the road leading to the field. Hurry!'

***

We left the field as we'd left home, stealing out through a gap in the fence. We moved into the bush again at a half trot. The singing slowly faded away as we put more distance between us and the field. When we could no longer hear it, we reduced our trot to a walk.

I asked myself why the soldiers were singing. It's a stupid hunter who sings when he's hunting. Sometimes people sing in loud voices when they're walking alone at night in order to scare off any bad spirits that might be lying in ambush – but were the soldiers scared of bad spirits?

We were not singing as we walked through the night; we were as silent as prey.

We walked through many maize fields and saw the shadows of cows grazing or heard the tinkle of bells. We still had not met anyone else and I asked mother why it seemed as if we were the only ones fleeing.

'I met many people running away from their homes when I was coming to look for you on the road to your school this afternoon. It seems such a long time ago…' Her voice faded away. Then, taking a deep breath, she added, 'Those who haven't been captured or killed are gone.'

'But where to?' I asked. I also wanted to know where we were going.

'Who knows?' mother answered. 'They might be hiding around us, waiting to return to their homes after the soldiers have left.'

I looked around but couldn't see anyone hiding in the bushes. I wondered if we also shouldn't stop and find a bush to hide in, but then I thought that mother knew better, and would take us to safety, just as she had always looked after me.

I almost asked her if she knew when the soldiers were going to go away, but I stopped myself as I felt that would be a stupid question. None of us knew. How could we know?

Auntie walked in silence behind me. Now and then I would look to see if she was still there – she was so quiet, but I knew it was the shock of everything that had happened to us. Somehow, I was thankful that walking and walking, putting one step in front of the other, had stopped me from thinking too much.

***

I had long lost count of time. I didn't even know where we were.

I'd even lost the feeling of distance, and was just plodding on behind mother.

Now and then we would stop for a few minutes to rest and drink water, and mother would breast-feed Gift, and then we would go on.

Much much later, a deep exhaustion started to creep over me. My feet felt heavy just as they had done when we'd first begun this journey, but I did not tell mother. I just kept on walking.

Then, miraculously, the sky began to lighten behind us. We had walked the whole night. We could see dew on the undergrowth. I could feel it making the bottom of my skirt, my legs and my shoes wet.

We walked on as the shadows melted from the trees. A low mist began rising from the ground, creeping under the bushes so it looked as though they were floating on clouds. It was a sort of dream world.

Then birds started calling, and daylight washed the countryside like a blessing. The mist evaporated, as if the land had just shrugged off sleep, and everything seemed normal. We walked on as the sunlight grew brighter and brighter, and soon it was hot again.

But, tired as we were, we did not stop, and I think the light of the morning gave us energy. Some time later, rain clouds started gathering in the sky, as it was almost the beginning of the rainy season.

I had never been this far before, but I knew that somewhere ahead of us was the Ngwizi River. The river is dry for a good part of the year, only filling during the rainy season. Although it's far away, when we approach from this direction, it winds down quite near our village to the north, which is where I learnt to swim.

At mid-morning mother said we must stop and have something to eat; we were all very very tired. We found a tree and sat in its shade. We had still not seen another soul. The clouds had dispersed and the sky was a clear blue.

We had *inkobe*, which was now very dry, and a stick of biltong each. Mother breastfed Gift again as we ate, not saying very much at all.

After eating, we drank some water, and then lay back in the shade. I immediately fell asleep, as if my world had suddenly shut down. But after what seemed like minutes, mother was shaking my shoulder to wake me up.

I sat up, rubbing my eyes. My whole body felt sore, and I was groggy with sleep.

'Auntie and I have decided that we will cross the Ngwizi River and go up into the Phezulu mountains, to hide there until all this is over.'

Despite my fatigue, I thought this sounded reasonable, because we couldn't walk on forever without a destination; and Bulawayo City was just too far away to reach on foot. It would be impossible to look for lifts on the road because of the soldiers.

Mother suddenly shushed us with a finger pressed to her lips. Her eyebrows were raised in alarm. I was still yawning and trying to clear the fog from my mind.

And then I heard the sound of feet running through the undergrowth ahead of us.

We all crouched down. Bushes surrounded the place where we were resting. I felt my skin crawl at the sight that met our eyes.

A group of four spirits had appeared out of the bushes, cutting across our path at a fast pace. They were only dressed in skirts made from grass and leaves. One of them carried another spirit on its back, which was white, and also dressed in a grass skirt. Streaks of blood ran down the back of this white spirit.

Chapter 14

Last year there was a traditional dance competition among all the secondary schools in the Kezi District. It was held at Maphisa Growth Point, which is the centre of the district. Our school participated, and we came third in the finals. Sithabile and I are members of the school dance team, and the dance teacher is Mr Mkandla, who is also the history teacher. We have a good dance uniform with skirts made from animal skins, which are reserved for special occasions. We do not use them during rehearsals. Instead we put on grass skirts that Mr Mkandla makes with our assistance for each rehearsal. We sometimes wear these skirts over our school uniforms as we are so proud to be part of the dance team.

I think it must have been because I was still so sleepy that I thought the figures before us were spirits; just a few minutes later, I recognised all of them. They were my teachers at Godlwayo Secondary school: Mr Ndlovu, our headmaster, Mr Bhebhe, the maths teacher, Mr Mkandla, and Miss Grant, the white woman, who teaches agriculture. It must have been Mr Mkandla who made them cover their nakedness with grass skirts, which was a good idea if you do not have any clothes. He was the one carrying Miss Grant on his back; her head was hanging to the side like a sleeping baby. Miss Grant is from Scotland. She arrived during the first term of this year to take up her job.

As we watched, the group came to a stop under a tree. Mr Mkandla placed Miss Grant on the ground, and the men all squatted around her. They seemed to be resting.

'Let's go over to them,' Auntie whispered.

'No,' mother whispered back. 'Let them go.'

'Maybe they know where they're going and there is safety there,' Auntie insisted.

Mother seemed to think a bit then she nodded her head.

'Okay, we will follow behind them when they leave, but at a distance. I don't want to us to be part of a crowd.'

'Don't be afraid, Mamvura,' Auntie said, as if reading mother's mind. 'You're our family, and Rudo is my daughter as she is my brother's child.'

It felt good to hear Auntie say this.

Mother shrugged her shoulders. 'Let's just wait until they leave and we'll follow them.'

'Okay,' Auntie said. It sounded as if she understood my mother's fears.

Then the men under the tree started cutting branches off bushes, and peeling off the bark. Mr Mkandla seemed to be the one giving orders. We watched them quickly make a stretcher. Then they placed Miss Grant on it, and a moment later, with Mr Mkandla and Mr Bhebe carrying the stretcher, they walked away, and the bush quickly swallowed them up.

***

Auntie always tells me stories before we go to sleep, especially on her drinking days. She used to drink a lot when she first came to live with us, more than she does now. Mother once told me that this was because she was unhappy with the way her marriage had turned out, but I was too young to understand how a bad thing can make somebody drink a lot of beer. I had always thought that beer was for happy people and this was why, when people were drunk, they danced and laughed a lot, or even sometimes fought each other from the excitement.

Just as she did to father, on those drinking days, Auntie sometimes tells me things that I have never heard her discuss with mother. I just listen silently as I know that Auntie would not be expecting me to say anything because, even if she is addressing me, she is really talking to herself.

She would tell me that she would never marry again because all men were untrustworthy, except for her brothers Genesis, my father, Innocent and Francis – especially Francis, she would add. I think she liked Uncle Francis more than her other brothers; perhaps because he was the only one who drank and would take her with him to Belinda's home for a drink.

She would also tell me that her husband had made a serious mistake when he married a lazy woman; one who only knew how to give birth but not how to work hard in the fields. She would say that now Sibanda, her former husband, regretted that he had treated her so badly, and that one day he would ask her to come back, but then she would tell him to *fokofo*. Auntie likes saying *fokofo* when she's had a drink, and she says it with relish. But, of course, Sibanda never came when she expected him. He came a year later, when Auntie was no longer drinking so much, and the response she gave him left mother and me in stitches.

***

Sibanda first sent his Uncle Mlilo to smooth the path for a talk with Auntie. Father was in Bulawayo, so when Mlilo arrived he asked to talk to mother. Afterwards, mother told Auntie that an uncle had been sent by Sibanda to ask her to return to her marriage and that Mlilo would come back the following afternoon for her reply. Then, he would talk to her himself, as he wanted Auntie to have enough time to prepare her answer.

'I will be ready for him,' Auntie told us.

Fortunately, it was school holidays so I was at home to witness an event I wouldn't have missed for the world.

In the morning, Auntie left home without saying anything to anybody and headed in the direction of Belinda's home. She returned later with a plastic container of beer, and shut herself in the spare bedroom, still without saying a word.

Later, we heard her singing and clapping her hands in the spare bedroom and I wondered if she was dancing alone, and asked mother if I could join her. Mother said no, Auntie was preparing herself for the meeting. I was happy for Auntie, thinking that she would soon find herself back with her husband.

However, it was not Mlilo who came but Sibanda himself. He was a short man with a big stomach and a face that reminded me of the pigs that Miss Grant bred in our school for our agriculture lessons. I knew Sibanda, as we visited his home in Dabulani village when Auntie was still married to him, but we had never been there after he married his second wife: Auntie had left him before we could do so, and so we'd never met the woman who caused her so much misery.

Sibanda was riding a bicycle, and he dismounted at our gate and stopped in the shade of the *mopane* tree. 'Can I please come in?' he saluted our home in a loud voice. I was just leaving the kitchen with a cup of sweetened *mahewu* for mother, who sat knitting on a reed mat in the shade of the bedroom hut. She was wearing her brown dress with white frills, which she reserves for special occasions. Father had bought it for her in the city at a garage sale held by a white woman who was leaving the country. I was also smart in a long yellow dress with white flowers, which father had bought for me on the same occasion.

'Come in, Baba Sibanda,' mother had responded.

'Please bring a chair for our visitor, Rudo.'

Auntie had come out of the spare bedroom at that precise moment, as if she'd been peeping through the window. She was wearing her short tiger dress, large dark sunglasses with round white frames, and an Afro wig. She stood at the door, and, placing her hand on her hip, struck a pose. I thought she looked like the model in a fashion magazine that Sithabile once showed me.

'Don't bother about the chair, Rudo, my child,' Auntie intervened. Then, she looked at Sibanda, who was wheeling his bicycle into the yard.

'Please stop right there,' she said, pointing a finger at him. 'Do not step into my brother's home. *Fokofo!*'

Mother's mouth fell open in surprise, but she did not say anything.

Sibanda took one look at Auntie, his lips set, and he continued wheeling his bicycle towards mother.

'I said, stop where you are right now, and step back!' Auntie yelled, still pointing at her former husband, 'Do you think this is your whorehouse?'

'Auntie!' mother interrupted, 'We have a child here. Please let us not use such language.'

But Auntie was beyond hearing. Screaming suddenly, she ran back into the spare bedroom. That took me by surprise. My first instinct was to follow her to comfort her, but a moment later she had burst out of the room again. This time she was carrying a knobkerrie with a very large head. Auntie's scream was fierce.

'Auntie!' mother called out and quickly stood up. Auntie, still yelling, raced towards Sibanda, the knobkerrie upraised.

Her husband had done a quick about-face. Turning his bicycle around, he leapt on it with amazing agility for a man of his size, and raced out of our gate. Seeing him fleeing, Auntie took aim and threw the knobkerrie at him with surprising force. It hit the rear wheel of the bicycle. 'Don't ever come back here again!' Auntie shouted after the disappearing form.

Mother was too astounded to speak, and I gazed at my aunt in astonishment. I knew she was tough, but I had not expected her to chase her husband out of the compound like a scrounging animal.

Auntie's expression was stormy. 'He thinks I'm a dog that eats its vomit,' she shouted. 'I will never do that. Never!' She shook a fist in Sibanda's direction. 'If you ever come back here again, I'm going to make you eat dust!'

She looked at us. 'He thinks that just because there are only women in this home, he can do whatever he wants to do. Never! Not when I'm around!'

Then she'd started laughing and I began to laugh with her. And mother couldn't keep a straight face and burst into a gale of laughter.

Then, Auntie returned to the spare room and came out with a container of beer.

'If anyone is looking for me, I'm going for a drink,' she said, and walked away in the direction of Belinda's home.

She returned the following day, wearing a cap over her wig, a cap which belonged to Mr Mkandla, my history teacher.

Chapter 15

I think it may have been Mr Mkandla who made Auntie chase her former husband away from our home. Two months previously, when I was leaving school on a Friday, Mr Mkandla had asked me to tell Auntie that he would be drinking at Belinda's home the following afternoon. It was the first time Mr Mkandla had asked me to do this. Until then, I did not even know that he knew Auntie. I gave my aunt the message, she thanked me, and I forgot about it.

But the following afternoon, Auntie took a long time dressing, and when she finally emerged from her room, mother asked rather pointedly, 'Are you going to the city, Auntie?'

Auntie was dressed in her special dress, the one with tiger stripes that clung to her body and stopped just above her knees. I'd only seen Auntie wear this dress once before, at Christmas when Uncle Francis had held a party and invited all the villagers. She was also wearing a pink sun hat, and had applied red lipstick.

'No, I'm going to Belinda's home,' Auntie replied.

'Who are you going with?' We all knew that Uncle Francis had gone to the city to sell his maize and would be back on Monday.

'I'm going alone,' Auntie said demurely. 'I will join other women there.'

Early the next morning, when I went to relieve myself outside, I saw Auntie coming through the gate in her tiger dress and pink hat. When she saw me she pressed her finger to her lips and disappeared into her room.

Still, I told mother that I'd seen Auntie coming home but all she said was, 'Auntie is an adult and she can do whatever she wants, even sleep out.'

I went back to sleep and forgot all about it.

***

The following Monday, Mr Mkandla's wife, who lives in the city, visited the school. Whenever she does so there is an atmosphere of excitement amongst the girls in our class, especially our group – Sithabile, Belinda, and Nobuhle. Mr Mkandla is our class teacher as well as being the history, and dance teacher. And there's a rumour that Miss Grant is Mr Mkandla's girlfriend because they're often seen together going to the borehole or walking slowly to Donga's store. We are careful to observe them for any signs of intimacy, and once we saw Miss Grant touch Mr Mkandla's hand as they walked around the school, adding fuel to the rumour. So whenever Mrs Mkandla arrives, we smell trouble for Mr Mkandla and Miss Grant. To add to the excitement, Mrs Mkandla spends time with Miss Grant: we watch them talking and smiling together, even in Mr Mkandla's presence. So, we think that Mr Mkandla is a very clever man as he is not only able to hide his affair with Miss Grant from his wife, but enables them to be friends. For this reason Mr Mkandla is one of our favourite teachers.

And on that very Monday, Mr Mkandla had given me a letter and asked me to give it to Auntie. He told me that I must show it to no one else, not even mother.

As I remembered what mother had told me, I gave the letter to Auntie and told no one. Thanking me, Auntie had also cautioned me not to tell anyone. She need not have bothered, as I didn't intend to; the last thing I wanted was a rumour about Auntie and Mr Mkandla. I did not even tell Sithabile.

Auntie could not read English but she can read and write a little Ndebele, though her handwriting is awful. I wondered what Auntie could make of Mr Mkandla's letter as I didn't think a teacher could write a letter in Ndebele, but Auntie never called me to read the letter for her, and so I did not know which language it was written in, or what it was all about, although I was intrigued.

The following morning, Auntie gave me a letter in another closed envelope for Mr Mkandla, stressing that it was our secret. I almost said that she should've asked me to write it for her as her handwriting was not fit to be read by a teacher. But I didn't and from that week I became the go-between as letters flowed between my teacher and my aunt in the coming months.

Chapter 16

It was easy to follow the spoor left by the teachers, as it contained a trail of blood. They seemed to be fleeing in a southerly direction, whilst we'd been heading east. 'Where do you think they might be going to, Auntie?' mother asked.

'I've no idea. Bulawayo is behind us, ahead are more villages, and then the Botswana border.'

Mother stopped walking.

'What is it?' Auntie asked. We had all stopped.

Mother was looking towards the east.

'Let's go where we decided to go first.'

'No, Mamvura,' Auntie said. 'Let us follow the teachers.' There was a pleading note in her voice.

'You said there are more villages towards the south, so the chances of meeting soldiers there will also increase,' mother said. 'But there are no villages to the east as far as the Ngwizi River; after that, there are just a few homes this side of Lotshe village which we can avoid. We can hide in the Phezulu mountains, while we consider what to do next, just as we planned. Let's think of the children.'

'Are you still afraid that people might not accept you and Rudo?'

Mother did not reply. Silence fell for a moment or two.

'Okay,' Auntie agreed finally. 'Let's go to the mountains. Then we can return later to our village and look for Rudo's father and Sithabile.'

So we changed course again. I saw Auntie take one last glance in the direction the teachers had taken but she did not say anything. I also wondered if she suspected what we suspected at school, that Miss Grant was Mr Mkandla's girlfriend.

***

Before we'd gone far, Gift woke up and started crying. Mother called for a rest so that she could breast-feed him. We sat in the shade of a bush, and while mother fed Gift, we had a meal of biltong and water. We still had *inkobe*, but we had to be careful to eat it a little bit at a time as it makes one thirsty and we had be careful with our drinking water. There was also the cabbage, but we hadn't touched that yet.

After Gift was satisfied, he started smiling at us, and despite the worry on her face, mother smiled back at him. I also smiled a bit although I was feeling very tired and did not really want to smile.

Then we lay down in the shade to rest, and I promptly fell asleep. I woke up much later with mother shaking my shoulder. Clouds had formed again, and they were darker and bigger now, as if the sky was growing angry. Mother had a worried frown on her face. 'We must move or the rain will catch us in the open,' she said.

We couldn't see anywhere to shelter from the rain but we stood up and moved on. My sleep had not rested me and I was still very tired, but I played a walking game to myself: counting your steps backwards from one hundred to zero and doing this over and over again. Now and then, there would be a flash of lightning and the distant rumble of thunder, as if huge volumes of water were swishing this way and that trying to find gaps in the clouds in order to fall to earth.

***

The first rains of the planting season are always met with excitement. When we're at home, and in better times, it's not surprising to see even the elders briefly dancing in rain, just to feel the drops fall on their skin. Children take off their clothes and run around in these first rains, letting the cool water wash over their bodies.

I will never forget the first rains of that spring.

We still had not found shelter when a huge raindrop splattered on my forehead. I looked up. Dark clouds filled the whole sky. And the earth was rich with the smell of rain and wet earth. We were crossing a bare patch of ground.

'This doesn't look good,' I heard mother saying. 'Why should it happen today of all days when we don't need the rain?'

Then she looked at me. 'Rudo, remove all the food from the plastic bag and give it to Auntie to put in the travelling bag.'

I looked at mother in surprise. If the food was removed from the plastic bag, it would be spoiled by the rain.

There was a moment of complete stillness as if we had walked into a pocket of silence. 'Please do as I say, Rudo.' Mother's voice was urgent. 'We have to make a raincoat for Gift to protect him.'

Then I understood. I removed the food from the plastic bag and gave it to Auntie. Mother took the bag, and using our knife, quickly fashioned a raincoat from it by cutting a hole at its top for the head and two holes for arms. She dressed Gift in the raincoat and he gurgled happily, thinking it was fun; then she tied him to her back again. Then the rain seemed to stop.

We walked on in expectant silence. We crossed a grove of *mopane* trees and went up a rise. The Phezulu mountains suddenly appeared to us for the first time on the horizon. Covered in a blue mist, they were still very far away, and there was the Ngwizi River to cross first and we could see no sign of it.

Then, the sky opened and it was suddenly pouring: large raindrops fell like stones on the head. Lightning zapped, and thunder boomed across the sky. We were still on the rise in an exposed space. Auntie quickly opened the travelling bag and took the pot out of it.

'Take the pot!' she cried out above the noise of the rain, offering the pot to mother. 'Cover Gift's head with it.'

Mother did so. She was holding the now helmeted Gift to her bosom.

'Let's move down and try to find a place to shelter!' mother shouted, and we quickly moved down the rise. A wind had sprung up and was driving the rain strongly against us so that we moved with our bodies bent forward. I tried to hold onto mother's skirt, for the strong wind was threatening to blow me away.

When we reached the bottom of the rise, the rain was falling even more heavily. It seemed as if a solid curtain of water had been dropped in front of us, and we couldn't see more than a few feet ahead. A large tree loomed out of the curtain, and mother moved towards it and stopped underneath it. A *mvagazi*, it had a thick trunk and foliage, but the rain was whipping in from the side and so it did not provide any protection. We moved around the tree and sought protection on the other side of the trunk. We were all crowded close together, although that seemed not to help us at all.

Then the wind suddenly changed direction and the rain was pelting us from the other side. We fled around the trunk of the tree yet again. Then I discovered that the trunk had a big hollow on its side at the height of my shoulders. Mother saw the hollow at the same time as I did, for she put her hand inside to feel it.

When she withdrew it, she was holding a big lizard by the tail. It was writhing furiously as it tried to escape. Mother threw it away into the rain as if it was an offering to the rain spirit.

Gift was crying. Mother reached inside the hollow again and I could see she was searching inside it for anything dangerous. Satisfied that there was nothing there, she took the pot off Gift's head and placed him in the hollow. Then she pressed her body against the mouth of the hollow, shielding it from the rain and the wind. I wished the hollow was big enough for all of us.

The tree was in a basin and water was steadily collecting at our feet as if we were standing in the middle of a very big river. I have never felt so miserable in all my life. I was also very cold, my teeth were chattering and I felt like crying. Then mother took me in her arms, and Auntie moved around my back putting her arms right round me, so that I was sandwiched between the two women. The rain seemed to increase, the lightning grew sharper, and the thunder deeper.

It was very easy to ask God why he was not looking on us kindly.

Chapter 17

At school, we've often been taught about the dangers of lightning, and how we should protect ourselves from it. Our teachers, from primary through secondary, have always taught us to avoid high places, and not to shelter under trees when there's a lot of lightning. When I was in Grade Four, two men in our village were killed by lightning walking through a grove of trees. When I was in Grade Seven, a family of five died when the hut they had been sheltering in during a rainstorm was struck by lightning. Our teachers also taught us how to make lightning conductors, and told us to teach our parents about how to use them. But in my home, I didn't have to teach father as he'd already installed lightning conductors in all our huts long before I learned about them.

As lightning flashed across the sky, my thoughts turned to a lightning strike. Would we be struck under this tree? I banished the thought from my mind. We already had enough to worry about. I reasoned that the tree, judging by its height and the size of its trunk, must have survived many storms. Surely it would not be struck today, just because we were crouching beneath it?

We huddled there for what seemed a lifetime. The rain fell hard that afternoon, as if it was trying to make up for the drought of the past two years. The water on the ground kept rising, and soon we were up to our shins in it. Mother kept checking on Gift, but he was kept quite dry in his hollow.

I wondered if we were in the middle of a flood. We've never had floods in the village, except once when the Ngwizi River burst its banks. Auntie heard my question even though I was not aware of asking it.

'It's not the Ngwizi River,' she said firmly. 'It's too far away from here. We're just in a hollow. If the water rises much more, we'll have to look for higher ground.'

The wind-lashed rain almost drowned out our voices.

'But we can also climb up the tree,' I said.

'We don't have to do that,' mother replied. 'We can go back the way we came until we reach the rise we were on before the rain started, but then we won't have the protection of the tree.'

A deep throbbing sound suddenly filled the sky, which I took for a prolonged roll of thunder. But instead of the sound fading away, it grew like thunder moving towards us.

'What's that?' Auntie asked.

'It's not water is it?' Mother was looking around, but the curtain of rain still surrounded us, and we couldn't see through it.

I was trying to gauge if we could reach the lower branches of the tree if another wave of water reached us, when Auntie whispered, 'It's a helicopter,' as if she was afraid it would hear us.

'It seems to be coming towards us,' mother added fearfully.

'Maybe it's the government coming to stop those wild soldiers.' There was a note of hope in Auntie's voice.

'If that happened, it would be very good,' mother replied.

I wished that this would be true, for it would mean the end to all this running and sadness.

The sound of the helicopter was now a powerful thumping in the sky that sent a thrill through my body.

Auntie must have been affected by the excitement too, for she ran from under the protection of the tree, splashing through the water. She stopped in the middle of the pouring rain and looked up at the sky.

'What are you doing Auntie?' mother shouted at her above the sound of the helicopter, which was still not visible.

'Maybe the helicopter will see us and we'll be saved,' Auntie shouted back. Her eyes were shielded from the rain by a hand.

The sound of the helicopter kept hammering toward us. Now it seemed as if it was right overhead, but it did not come into sight. Then an amplified voice boomed out, almost as if was God speaking over the rain. 'You are surrounded by the army.' The message was chilling. It was speaking in Shona. 'Go back to Mbongolo Primary School at once.'

'Auntie!' I heard mother call. 'Run!'

But Auntie was still looking up at the sky, towards the voice and the clatter of the helicopter, and she did not move. I knew she had not understood the words. I broke free from mother and rushed to her through the water. She was still looking up at the sky, a terrible look on her rain-washed face, one of a deep hope but also of knowing she was probably wrong.

'It's those soldiers, Auntie!' I shouted at her, grabbing her hand.

She looked at me in incomprehension. 'It's the bad soldiers!' I yelled again.

Then the voice repeated its message, now in Ndebele. 'You are surrounded by the army. Go back to Mbongolo Primary School at once.'

Auntie was still looking up at the sky. There was a look of utter disbelief on her face, but she didn't move. I pulled hard on her hand. The helicopter was above us now, although we couldn't see it over the rain, and that terrible voice seemed to be booming right inside my heart.

'There's nowhere to hide, people of Saphela area,' the voice continued with its message in Ndebele. The voice was clearer now, and heavily accented. 'Go back to the primary school at once and we will forgive you.'

Auntie snapped out of her trance. I felt her tugging my hand sharply, and we fled towards mother, hand in hand. Water was flying everywhere as our feet splashed through the torrent and the rain hammered down. I looked up briefly before we reached the tree. Nothing was visible in the sky, just an empty watery greyness. Then the sound of the helicopter was swallowed up and it finally disappeared, leaving behind it the rumble of thunder as the storm raged on.

Chapter 18

Then, just as suddenly as it had started, the rain stopped. A deep silence followed, broken by the plop of raindrops falling from the tree onto the puddles. There was water as far as the eye could see all around us.

The few remaining clouds were all racing southwards, as if they wanted to break over every dry place before darkness. I was so wet I felt I would never become dry again, and I felt cold to my bones.

Then the sun broke through the dispersing clouds and it was so bright that it dazzled my eyes. Frogs miraculously began croaking all around us, as if they had fallen from the sky with the rain.

Mother reached into the hollow in the tree, and lifted Gift out. He was awake, and he was smiling, as if he had been having a good time with the lizards. He reached out to me as though to comfort me. Although I was shivering and felt miserable, I took his little hand and talked some baby talk to him. Then mother said we must move on to higher ground and find a place where we could dry ourselves.

We moved away from the tree, splashing through the water, still heading in the direction of the Phezulu mountains. The travelling bag that Auntie carried on her head was soaked through and dripped water down her neck.

We walked out of the water onto a stretch of mud. The going was tough as the mud was slippery and stuck on our shoes, making our feet heavy.

Eventually we came to the top of a sandy rise. Beyond it, the land fell away to another stretch of muddy ground. The clouds had cleared, and the sun was shining imperturbably. Ahead of us, the Phezulu mountains sat low on the horizon, like they were the end of the world.

We stopped on the rise. Mother lifted Gift out of his plastic coat. His clothes were damp and mother stripped him naked. There was nothing we could do about our wet clothes as all those in the travelling bag were soaked through, but Auntie opened the bag and removed the food, which had been reduced to a paste. She gave it to me and I wrapped it back in the plastic bag, and then tied the bag with bark so that it was a tight roll, which I could carry on my head.

Then, under the hot sun, with mother carrying the naked Gift in her arms, we continued with our flight.

***

During the war, our Freedom Fighters had a secret camp in the Phezulu mountains, where they regularly held evening *pungwes* which villagers attended. Father went there several times. He always told mother before he went, and it took him a week to get back home again. Mother had never gone to any of these *pungwes*.

One day, after the war, father told us about them and what they did there. They sounded like exciting occasions where adults sang and danced with the Freedom Fighters, and ate food that had been brought in by women from nearby villages. Father also told us that the location of the *pungwes* was kept very secret so that they would not be known to the Smith soldiers.

These were the mountains that we were now trying to reach. Just as they had given Freedom Fighters protection during the long years of struggle, this time we hoped that they would give us protection from the soldiers ravaging the villages.

Looking at the hazy mountains, knowing they were still so far away, was very depressing, as the bluish haze was a reflection of the vast distance we still had to cover, and also the insecurity that faced us.

I thought about my father, wondering where he was and what was happening to him right now. I prayed silently that he was still alive; then the image of Chief Mabhena's sawn-off hand came to me, and a great terror descended on me. It was only when I looked at the figure of mother with Gift on her back struggling forward through the mud that I was comforted. It was also comforting to know that Auntie was walking behind me.

The sun was still climbing, and our shadows were now directly beneath us. Then we got through the last of the mud and began crossing firm ground. My school uniform was dry from the sun, but I almost wished it was wet again as it was so hot. Mother's eyes constantly searched the sky, and I guessed that she was on the look out for the helicopter.

At last, I told mother that I was tired and wanted to rest.

'Let's drink some water and move on,' she replied. 'We can't rest now. It's too early. We have to cross the river first.'

We stopped and drank some water, then mother breast-fed Gift, and we continued on our journey.

Mother had tied Gift to her back again, but because he was still naked, she had placed a branch of green leaves over his head to protect it from the sun. Gift was silent, and I thought he was asleep and envied him, but when I drew closer I saw that he was wide awake and that his eyes were peeping at me through his leaf hat.

The vegetation was becoming thicker, and greener. We now moved under tall bushes and trees that protected us from the sun. This felt much better, and I guessed the Ngwizi River must be nearer, and a little while later, I was proved right. We broke out of the bush and onto the banks of the river.

Chapter 19

The Ngwizi is a big river. For the past two years at the point where it passes behind my home, the bed has been reduced to a wide belt of sand pockmarked by rocks and the trunks of dead trees. The breadth of the river was the same here too, except that today there was water flowing in it, although the level was very low.

Before we walked down the bank, mother picked up a long, stout stick from the ground. 'Give the food to Auntie to put in the bag so that your hands are free.' Mother was hefting the stick. She was going to sound the water with it as we crossed.

I gave the plastic bag of food to Auntie.

'Let's take off our shoes and put them in the bag too,' Auntie said, and we did that as well. We didn't even think twice about having our food in the same bag as our shoes and clothes.

The water was muddy and seemed still. Halfway down the bank, there was a line of foam on the sand, where the water had flowed during the storm. I looked up the river. On the horizon a curtain of fine dark lines seemed to be connecting the earth and the sky like the fine threads on a banana.

'It's still raining over there,' mother said. 'Let's cross quickly, the water might rise at any minute.'

Mother dipped her stick into the water. In her other hand she also held our water container. The water didn't seem very deep, or the current too strong. Then she put one leg into the water, which came up to her knee. She was still for a moment, with one leg on the bank, and the other in the water.

Mother then stepped into the water with both feet. I was watching her carefully, fearing that the river might wash her away. Then mother instructed me to get into the water behind her and hold on to her skirt. Auntie followed me.

I stepped into the water, which came up to my waist. Then we moved forward.

The water was cool, and the current felt strong against my legs, but not strong enough to wash me away.

Now that we were in the water, the river seemed wider. Foam, grass and branches swirled around us as we struggled forward.

The further we walked into the river, the deeper it became. The water was now up to my chest, and I noticed that it was up to mother's waist, though Gift's feet on her back were still slightly above the water. Then I felt the current grow stronger.

'I think there's a flash flood coming our way,' Auntie shouted. 'Hurry.'

I was now holding on to mother's dress at waist level as her skirt was now submerged.

'Hurry, Rudo!' I felt mother increase her pace. I tightened my grip on her skirt and tried to move a little faster, as the current pushed against us like a live creature. More foam and flotsam were flowing past. Then mother stopped moving, and I saw her gasp in shock. She was looking upriver. I saw it also, and I felt my heart trip. But it was not an incoming flood.

A naked body was floating towards us. We had all stopped moving and stared at it in silence. The body was headed straight between mother and me. As if the sight of the body was not shocking enough, I saw that it did not have a head, only a neck with a big open wound at the top. I quickly let go of mother's dress, and the body floated past between us. We all watched it disappear down the river.

'Just forget about it,' I heard mother say. 'Let's go.'

The words were hardly out of her mouth when, without warning, the water gave a powerful surge, and I found myself swirling beneath it. I couldn't see anything, and I couldn't get back on my feet. It seemed as if a powerful hand was whirling me round and around. Although I can swim, the surge of water was too powerful for me. Then my head broke out of the river, I quickly inhaled some air, before I was dragged under water again. I opened my eyes as I whirled, but I couldn't see anything, except for flashes of white, then darkness, then whiteness again. I panicked. The current was too powerful. I felt I was going to drown. But sense told me not to open my mouth and scream, and I held my breath tightly. Then I felt my body jerk to a sudden stop, and my head was out of the water again.

**

Water was roaring all around me. The sun was a fuzzy burning disc. I was gasping for air. I expected to be pulled back under the water again, and I screamed. But nothing happened. My head was still above water, which was rushing past me. I tried to move, but I couldn't. Then I realised that my uniform skirt was hitched at the hem by the root of a tree that projected into the water from the bank. The water was tearing past the roots, and foam was rising up and being deposited on them too. I tried to stand up, but the current was too strong. Then, above the thundering of the water, I heard a powerful roaring in the sky, and a voice booming down.

'You are surrounded by the army.' It was the same voice in heavily accented Ndebele. 'Go back to the primary school at once and you will be forgiven.' The message was repeated again, and then, oddly, rhumba music started playing through the air. Then the helicopter thundered past above me, briefly eclipsing the sun, and disappeared, taking the loud party music with it.

I looked around. The bank was overhung by trees. Their roots projected into the water like a mat. I gripped one of them tightly with one hand, and pulled hard at my skirt with the other. It suddenly tore free as the current flung my feet away, but I was clinging tightly to the root with both hands and so I was not swept away. Then slowly I pulled myself out of the water and onto the bank. My heart was beating so hard I thought it would burst out of my chest.

I didn't know which bank I was on, whether it was the one we'd been coming from, or the one we'd been moving towards. I walked further up the sand of the bank, which emerged into bushes at the top.

Ahead of me were the Phezulu mountains. I'd been washed away. But there was no sign of mother, Auntie or Gift.

I looked back at the river. It's water was roaring past the point from which I had emerged, and I knew I'd been very lucky that my skirt had been snagged tightly, otherwise I would've been washed away. Could mother, Auntie, and Gift be still in the water? Nobody sucked down the angry river could ever hope to come out of it alive. I'd been lucky. But what was I going to do now?

And then my heart leapt. A voice was calling my name. Mother's voice. Auntie's voice echoed it. I shouted back, and they called again, and I discovered that they were also on my side of the river, although I couldn't see them.

'Stay where you are!' mother called. 'We're coming to you!'

I didn't move. Then Auntie emerged from the bushes by the bank in front of me, still with our bag of clothes on her head. Behind her was mother. And then I noticed that mother did not have Gift tied on her back. I was aghast.

When mother reached me she hugged me tightly.

'I can't find Gift,' she said. She was almost in tears. 'There was a flash flood. Let's follow the bank and pray that he's still alive.'

I noticed that she'd also lost the water container, but at this moment it didn't matter at all.

A new sense of shock seemed to hang over us, even heavier than the one I'd felt when I'd first seen the cooked bodies in Uncle Genesis's burned bedroom.

We walked down the riverbank, carefully inspecting the edge where it met the water, the thick roots that projected into the river, and the bushes that hung over it. My heart was in my mouth. I remembered the force of the water that had knocked me over; I could still feel myself whirling underwater, helpless in the grip of the flash flood. How could Gift survive that? Could he have met with luck just as he'd escaped the fire in his home, or just as my skirt had been snagged by the root, for isn't it said in our culture that babies carry luck with them?

72

There was no Gift on the bank. The other bank was too far away, and it was impossible to cross the river again as the current was still far too strong, but from the little we could see, there seemed to be no sign of Gift there either.

Our mood was very heavy. Something priceless had been taken from us, something that had become the centre of our lives in our flight for salvation; a hope that we felt we wouldn't be able to live without. Continuing with our journey now felt empty and hopeless. I didn't think I wanted to continue, but felt I would search the river and the bank until we found out what had happened to Gift, no matter how long this took.

After some time of walking and searching along the bank, mother suddenly raised her hand for silence, her head cocked attentively. My eyes immediately went to the sky, searching for sound. Instead of the sound of a helicopter, the cry of a child drifted downwind.

'Did you hear that?' Auntie's voice was hushed.

Mother did not reply, but plunged ahead through the bushes, with us scurrying behind her. My heart in my mouth, I prayed it was Gift and not a trick of the river sounds. We broke through a clump of bushes, and then we all came to a surprised stop, panting hard.

A short distance away, a man was standing on a low slab of rock, looking at the river. He had a naked child in his arms, and it was this child that was crying. The man's figure seemed familiar. We hurried over to him. I prayed that the baby that he was holding was Gift. Auntie was the first to recognise the man even before we reached him.

'Uncle Ndoro!' she cried out. My heart leapt as I also recognised that the baby he was carrying was Gift.

Uncle Ndoro's eyes were fixed on the angry water, and he gave no indication that he'd seen us, or heard Auntie's voice. Gift was crying. The shrill noise echoed over the water. I looked briefly at the river, expecting to see something there that Uncle Ndoro was staring at, like a floating body, but there was nothing.

'That's our baby, Uncle Ndoro,' mother said, when we reached him. Gift reached out towards mother, crying even more loudly.

'Oh, thank you, God,' Auntie's voice was full of a thankfulness that overwhelmed us all.

'Where did you find him, Uncle Ndoro?'

But he continued to hold the yelling, struggling Gift close to his chest, while looking intently at the river. His lips were moving softly, though no sound came out of them.

Then we heard the dreaded noise again. A helicopter approaching.

Mother reached out for Gift again, and then Uncle Ndoro spoke: 'I'm looking for my bus. Can somebody please tell me where it is?'

The sound of the helicopter's throbbing engine increased. And with it came the incongruous rumba music. Mother quickly took Gift from Uncle Ndoro.

'Lie down!' Mother shouted at us, and she dropped into a crouch. We were all on exposed ground.

We quickly fell flat, but Uncle Ndoro remained standing, his eyes on the river. The sound of the helicopter seemed to be right on top of us, although we could not see it through the trees. Then the music was switched off, and the amplified voice boomed down again.

'We have you surrounded,' it said in its terrible Ndebele accent. 'Go back to the primary school at once and you will come to no harm.'

'Let's hide over there!' mother shouted again. She was pointing at some thick bushes on the bank whose foliage hung into the river. We sprinted for them.

The water under the bushes was not deep and neither was it flowing strongly at this point. The overhanging foliage covered us from the sky.

Then the helicopter broke through the trees on the opposite bank. It was flying very low. The same rumba music danced over the water.

Uncle Ndoro had not followed us. He was standing where we'd found him, still looking at the river, intently examining something we couldn't see. He did not even look up at the helicopter, or give any indication that he'd seen or heard it.

The machine was hovering over the river, an ugly looking beast in army colours. It seemed to be facing us; there was a soldier standing at each of its doors behind big guns with long barrels. Two other men sat behind the front window. The helicopter was flying so low that I could see them clearly. One was the soldier in the large spectacles that I'd met on the road from school when Uncle Ndoro's bus had crashed. It was only yesterday, but it seemed an impossibly long time ago. As I gazed at him, he raised a pair of binoculars to his eyes, and looked directly towards our hiding-place.

Chapter 20

One of my favourite games is hide-and-seek. We play it a lot after the harvest season when there's less work to do in the village. On moonlit nights, all the children of the Jamela clan liked to go to Uncle Genesis's home where we divide into age groups and play our separate games until the adults call us home to sleep. I've always enjoyed hiding and have others fail to find me, especially when they come close and I can see them but they can't see me. Then I come into the open and declare that I've won that round.

But that day, as we crouched under the bushes on the banks of the Ngwizi River, it was a different story. It was not a game of hide-and-seek, but a matter of life and death.

I don't know why the soldier with the binoculars didn't see us. Sometimes I think he did, but realising that we were the Shona-speaking people he'd spared before, decided to give us another chance. We shall never know.

The helicopter banked to the right. Now one of the soldiers with a gun at the door of the aircraft was looking straight at Uncle Ndoro. He seemed to stare at him as if surprised to see anyone standing still and not immediately turning to flee. Then the music was suddenly switched off and everything appeared to freeze. Even the water appeared to stop flowing. The roar of the helicopter was the only thing that seemed to exist: a powerful thump-thump-thump that felt a part of the roof of the sky.

The spectacled soldier peered down through a side window at Uncle Ndoro though his binoculars.

Then there was a mind-numbing explosion, which became a single tight roar. The soldier behind the gun was shooting at Uncle Ndoro who, with two great bounds, leapt into the river. I watched him hit the water and disappear. The soldier swung his gun towards the river, still shooting. I saw no sign of Uncle Ndoro in the brown, swift-flowing current.

Then the helicopter spun around again with its tail towards our hiding place. It hung over the river like a dragonfly, and I guessed the soldier with spectacles was searching the water through his binoculars. Then, it moved slowly down the river and around a bend. We watched it until it became a small speck, like a mosquito, before it disappeared.

***

We remained under the bushes for a little while after the helicopter had disappeared.

'Do you think Uncle Ndoro was hit?' Auntie asked.

'Who knows?' mother replied. They were speaking in low voices. 'But what I know is that he seems to have lost his mind.'

'We have to try and find him,' Auntie said. 'He saved Gift for us.'

'Let's wait a bit here,' mother said. 'That helicopter might come back.'

We subsided into silence. The sounds of the river were all around us: the gurgle of water and the croak of frogs.

'The soldier with binoculars is the one who ordered the killing of Uncle Genesis and Francis,' mother said. 'He's the one who took away Rudo's father.'

'And he's the one we met on the way from school,' I added.

'The one who ordered the nurses to strip naked before he took them away in the army truck.' Auntie's voice sounded strange.

'I heard the soldiers calling him Captain Finish,' mother said.

'So he's come to finish us all off,' Auntie said. 'But why?'

'Only God knows,' mother replied. 'But he'll be judged in heaven together with all those who've assisted him.'

Then the sound of the helicopter returned again, growing louder and louder, although we couldn't see it. The rumba music was now playing at full blast, as if the soldiers were celebrating the discovery of Uncle Ndoro's body.

Then we saw it again: a speck that grew into a fly, then a bird, eventually becoming the helicopter again. It turned at the bend in the river channel, and seemed to be looking straight at us again like a giant angry dragonfly with a single glass eye.

We crouched frozen under the bushes. The helicopter hovered over the spot where Uncle Ndoro had jumped into the river. I could see Captain Finish. He was searching the bank on the other side of the river with his binoculars. Then, as if impatient, the helicopter gave a great roar, lifted into the sky, banked, and sped away towards the north and Mbongolo village.

Behind it trailed the echo of its thundering engine and the raucous sound of rumba music played too loudly.

Chapter 21

After the helicopter had disappeared, we waited. The water was receding. We were silent, even Gift on mother's back, who was gripping my finger in his small hand. Even the river seemed to have fallen silent.

After a while, mother said we could climb out of the water and away from the screen of bushes that had sheltered us from death.

The sun still shone brightly and the ground on the bank seemed almost dry, as if it had not rained so heavily just a few hours ago.

'Let's see if we can find Uncle Ndoro,' Auntie said, her eyes casting around.

We followed the bank for a while, just as we'd done when we'd been searching for Gift. We walked along its edge, our eyes searching the bushes and the water. The water level seemed to have dropped. Auntie was walking in front. She seemed the most determined to find Uncle Ndoro, as if this one act, successfully completed, would provide her with an answer. Turning a bend, with an exclamation of horror she moved quickly towards a body that lay half in and half out of the water, its head stuck in a clump of bushes. We drew nearer and recoiled when we realised that it had no head – I thought it must be the body that had floated past us just before the flash flood, because this one was also naked, and a man.

We quickly turned away without a word, as if explanations would increase the brutal reality. I wondered if its head had been cut off by a person or been bitten off by a crocodile. Then mother spoke.

'If the bullets hit Uncle Ndoro, his body will have been taken away by the current and we can never hope to find it.' I could hear the dejection in her voice suggesting that our search was futile and that we must continue our journey towards the Phezulu mountains. Auntie stopped. 'You're right.' She looked hard at the river, then she turned towards the mountains and said, 'Let's go.'

There was defeat in her voice.

***

Once we'd left the banks of the river, the ground was almost bare of vegetation, save for a few trees here and there.

Our clothes were still wet but we'd all removed our shoes from the bag and swung them from our hands to help them dry. Gift was fast asleep on mother's back. I could hardly believe that this little boy had been through so much and survived.

After walking through thick sand that sucked at our feet and made movement a hard slow task, just as the mud had done earlier, our clothes dried quickly.

We reached an open stretch of rocky ground whose length and width was almost the size of two football fields and came to a stop beside a bush. In the middle of the clearing we could see a white person lying on the ground. The body was naked like the ones we'd seen at the river. Beside it stood two motionless vultures, their heads lowered, as if contemplating unpleasant thoughts.

'Let's walk around the clearing,' mother said. Her eyes were on the body. 'We might be seen by the helicopter if it returns.' I noticed that even though her eyes were on the body, she spoke as if she hadn't seen it.

Auntie nodded in agreement.

'But mother…' I said.

'What?'

'There's somebody lying there.'

Mother sighed. There was a brief silence, broken by the crackle of dry grass around us.

'It's a dead body, Rudo,' mother said finally. 'Look, there are vultures beside it.'

'Maybe it's Miss Grant.'

'Maybe it is,' mother said. 'But even if it is, there's nothing we can do for her.'

'I'm going to see who it is,' Auntie said, placing the travelling bag down beside me.

* * *

During those moonlit nights when we played hide-and-seek around Uncle Genesis's home, the best way not to be discovered was to constantly change hiding-places, while making sure that you didn't stray far, as we believed that there were goblins waiting to capture children at night.

Changing hiding-places without being discovered requires skill. One has to watch the movement of the seekers without being seen, and keep trying to find a way of moving to a place that they've already searched. This sometimes requires a quick dash across an open space behind their backs.

With one quick look at the sky, Auntie sped across the clearing towards the body. Our eyes were on her as I held my breath. She had pulled up the hem of her skirt so we could see her legs flying behind her.

When she was halfway across the clearing, the two vultures rose into the air on sluggish wings and clumsily settled on the top of a tree on the other side.

Auntie reached the body, and knelt beside it. Then she ran back towards us. Everything happened very quickly. A shadow flitted across the clearing in front of Auntie. I saw her look up at the sky in mid stride, as I did so also.

'More vultures,' mother said. Two more vultures were circling overhead.

Then Auntie reached us. She took a moment to catch her breath.

'Yes, it's the white teacher,' she said. 'She's dead. She has several bullet wounds on her back.'

'May her soul rest in peace,' mother murmured.

'I saw the teachers' tracks, now they're heading for the mountains, too.'

Chapter 22

Although fear had stopped us feeling tired, I now felt as if my feet would give away under me as we left the clearing behind us. I estimated we'd been walking for nearly three hours, since we'd left the river. I'd never walked for so long at one go in my life. Now and then we would make quick stops for mother to breast-feed Gift, and then we would go on walking.

I was also very thirsty. My tongue felt dry and rubbery. Since we had lost the water container, we were dependant on finding a spring. Then Gift started crying. Mother walked on, her hand gently patting his back.

'Please be quiet, Gift,' she murmured soothingly. 'We can't stop now. Shsh baby, shsh.'

But her words did not quieten the little boy, and his cry became a continuous wail. I moved nearer mother and also began patting his back. His cry became a whimper, but it didn't stop. We walked on. The Phezulu mountains appeared and disappeared as if they were teasing us as we climbed up and down the valleys. Then we came across another dead body lying half hidden in short grass. Mother urged us to walk on without looking at it.

'Not one of the teachers,' I heard Auntie say as we walked past it.

***

Godlwayo Secondary has four blocks of buildings each with three classrooms, and each form has a block of its own. There are still not enough classrooms for the school enrolment, so we have hot-seating. We had five teachers in the school and some doubled, or even trebled, their lessons. The teachers all lived in cottages inside the school near the orchard. As I thought about this, I knew that things would never be the same again.

My father also did his schooling at Godlwayo Secondary, a long time ago in the early seventies. At that time it had only one classroom and two teachers. The present four blocks of buildings were built in 1981 when I was in Grade Seven at Mbongolo Primary.

I wondered if the soldiers had also burned down my school since the teachers had fled, and I wondered how they'd managed to escape.

Although Auntie had said that the men in front of us were heading for the mountains, I doubted it, because most of our teachers came from the city. Maybe they hoped to walk over the mountains and on to the city. It is very far away – about six hours by bus past the mountains. I don't know how far that is on foot.

I also wondered if mother's fear of the teachers was well-founded. Would they hold her to account because she was Shona? I tried to comfort myself that they were educated people, and educated people do not do such things. Educated people are taught to love and respect others, and that is what they teach us. They even had had a white person in the school though during the war we were fighting against whites. And Mr Mkandla also wrote letters to Auntie, an uneducated village woman. Teachers did not discriminate. I hoped mother was making a mistake.

***

We were nearing Lotshe village. The bush was becoming denser again and there were more trees. This area of the village, which can be seen from the Saphela road to the south, does not have homesteads. They are found to the east on the other side of the Phezulu mountains. We were following one of the many footpaths that criss-crossed the valley, which seemed to lead towards the mountains.

To relieve our thirst, we would stop now and then to uproot the young shoots of **umvimila** trees, which were plentiful, and chew on them. Still it was not enough to quench my deep thirst, which had begun to make me feel dizzy.

Then we passed one of the large fearful holes in the ground that was once Saphela Gold Mine. It is no longer in use but there is a tower of rusted machinery beside the mineshaft and behind that a huge mound of earth. There are two such mounds in this area, although we had yet to pass the second. I'd seen them from Saphela road when I was travelling along it by bus.

'I'm glad that we're walking through here in daylight,' mother said. 'It would be very easy to fall down one of these shafts at night.'

I agreed with her, but I didn't have the heart to reply because I was so tired.

***

Finally, and after what seemed a lifetime, we reached the bottom of the mountain. It was late afternoon and the sun was on the other side of the slope, so we were in shadow. The range was huge, rolling into the distance as if there was no end to it.

Mother said we must rest before beginning our ascent. We moved off the path and found a big shady tree surrounded by a circle of bushes that would hide us.

'I know you're very thirsty, Rudo,' mother said, 'we'll find water on the mountain.' She began breast-feeding Gift and went on, 'I remember your father telling me that when they attended the *pungwes* there were fresh water springs there.'

'Mountains always have water,' Auntie added. I was so thirsty and dizzy that I wondered if they were just saying this to comfort me: I knew my feet had been dragging on the ground, though I hadn't complained.

Thirst is a very bad thing. It can stop you thinking about anything else. But sometimes you can forget about it, like when you want to wee-wee in a bus and have to wait for a bus stop. I was holding my thirst like that: sometimes it would wash painfully over me, and sometimes, if I thought really hard about something else, it would just disappear. But I knew a time was coming when the need to drink would swallow me and I would not be able to control it, and then I didn't know what would happen.

I tried to smile at Auntie, but I felt my lips crack and tears flood my eyes. I quickly looked away, pushing the tears back – and just at that moment there was a sharp cracking sound in the bushes.

We all froze.

Chapter 23

When you are frightened, a sudden sharp sound can steal all the energy from your body, and make you feel that anything can catch you.

Another cracking sound followed the first one. My eyes were on mother. She was frantically signalling that we must lie down flat. Gift was still suckling from her breast, and was silent.

We all lay on the ground, mother lying sideways with Gift nestled to her breast so he didn't make a noise. I could see through the bushes in the direction of the crackling of crushed leaves. Mother and Auntie were looking that way too. A pair of dark boots emerged from behind one of the bushes, which was so high and thick that it concealed the rest of the intruder's body. We hardly dared breathe.

The boots walked around the bush. Mother gasped. The man was Uncle Ndoro.

***

He walked towards our hiding place heading in a direction that would have taken him right past us. I could see him clearly. The sky was very blue behind his head. I was astonished that he was still alive. Gift had escaped death twice but he was a baby and babies were blessed just like I said before. I couldn't imagine a grown-up surviving that hail of bullets from the helicopter. And I couldn't imagine that a person who seemed not himself would be able to walk all this way and know where to come.

For a brief moment I thought we were looking at a ghost. I think our surroundings contributed to that feeling: the sunlit green bushes, the clear sky, the silence of the forest broken by the trill of cicadas. I felt a sense of unreality – just as I had when we'd seen the teachers running naked but for their skirts of leaves and I'd thought for a moment that they were spirits.

When Uncle Ndoro reached our hiding-place, he stopped. I don't know why, and I could only see his profile. His lips were moving, just as they had when we'd last seen him at the river, holding Gift.

I looked at mother, and she motioned with a finger pressed to her lips that I must remain very still. She was not looking at Uncle Ndoro but behind him at the bushes from which he'd emerged.

I looked at Uncle Ndoro again. He'd not moved, but his lips were moving, as if he was casting a spell, or wanted to say something that was refusing to come out of his mouth. I noticed blood on the right side of his overalls top, but he didn't show any signs of pain, not on his face, or in the way he held his body.

Satisfied that nobody was following him, Mother rose to her knees. I looked up at her, but she motioned that Auntie and me should stay hidden. She handed the sleeping Gift to Auntie. Then she stood up and walked over to Uncle Ndoro.

'Are you all right, Uncle Ndoro?' I heard her ask. She was standing in front of him. They're about the same height, although mother has the bigger body. Uncle Ndoro did not reply, but his lips moved. Then mother took his hand and led him to us.

Auntie and I were sitting up when she reached us. She asked Uncle Ndoro to sit in the shade besides us, and he did so without a word. Auntie handed Gift to me and she leaned forward and opened the buttons of Uncle Ndoro's bloodied overalls. We found a deep scratch oozing blood .

'How did you get that, Uncle Ndoro?' Auntie asked, her voice loud as if she was speaking to someone with an understanding problem.

Mother was looking at Uncle Ndoro's wound. 'Maybe a bullet grazed his skin,' she said. 'Are you hurt anywhere else?'

'Has anybody seen my bus?' Uncle Ndoro responded tonelessly. 'I can't find it anywhere.'

'Your bus crashed on Saphela road,' mother said, in a raised voice. 'It's there beside the road and you'll see it when we return.'

But Uncle Ndoro gave no indication that he'd heard her.

'He must have had a bad knock on his head during the accident,' mother said. 'I wonder if he can even see us.'

Auntie waved a hand in front of Uncle Ndoro's eyes, the way you do if you want to wake up somebody who has fainted. 'Can you see me, Uncle Ndoro?' she asked, but he just stared straight ahead.

Then Auntie and mother helped Uncle Ndoro out of his overall top and inspected his chest, satisfying themselves that he had no other wounds. There was no blood on his trousers and he walked without a problem, so they thought his legs were all right too. Then Auntie helped him put on his top again.

While mother and Auntie fussed over him, Uncle Ndoro just stared into space. I wondered if he had been following us without knowing it or if he had just found us by chance.

Mother took the food out of the clothes bag. It was still wet. She carefully separated the biltong from the *inkobe*, and then she broke off pieces of *inkobe* and gave us each some. She was just offering some to Uncle Ndoro, when he suddenly stood up and walked away. Auntie leapt up and ran after him. She grabbed his arm and led him back to us.

'Sit down Uncle Ndoro,' Auntie was saying. 'Sit down Baba, we will find your bus.' She was persuasive. Uncle Ndoro obeyed, although I didn't think he understood what she was saying. Auntie took the *inkobe* that mother had tried to give to Uncle Ndoro, and gave it to him. He just looked at the food, as if he did not know what it was.

'He's become ill,' Auntie said. She was looking at him as one would look at one's own sick child. I looked at Uncle Ndoro's head, knowing I'd seen blood on it at the crash site. Despite all the time he'd spent in the river, there was still clotted blood above his ear. I pointed it out to Auntie and she examined his head. There was a deep cut there, which had been partially concealed by his hair. There was no blood seeping from the cut, but it glistened wetly.

'It looks very bad,' mother said. 'I think this knock is the one that's made him lose his senses. Let's hope he regains them soon.' She was gently rocking Gift in her arms. Auntie sat beside Uncle Ndoro, who had his legs spread out before him.

Mother woke Gift up and breast-fed him, then she said it was time to move on again.

Chapter 24

This time Gift was singing on mother's back when we moved off, as if he hadn't a care in the world. It was not a song really but gentle baby noises that were satisfying to hear. Tired as I was, his little voice gave me something comforting to hang on to.

We'd put on our shoes again, as they were dry. I was still walking behind mother, with Auntie behind me. She was leading Uncle Ndoro by the hand, to make sure we did not lose him again.

We were now walking up the hill, and the going was very tough, so we walked slowly. We had to be careful where we placed our feet, for the faint path had loose stones on it and it would have been very easy to slip and fall. We seemed to toil upwards forever. Then the path grew even steeper, and sometimes it was only safe to crawl, pulling ourselves from rock to rock. Auntie could no longer hold Uncle Ndoro's hand, but he still followed behind her. Occasionally, he would just stop as if he could not go on and Auntie would coax him to continue walking.

Now and then I looked behind me. The higher we climbed, the more the countryside stretched away below. I sometimes caught brief glimpses of landmarks we'd passed: the mounds of earth beside the two mineshafts looked like the breasts of a woman. The land seemed to end with the river's dense green tree line. To the left, the big Saphela road wound like a ribbon; the older smaller road was like thread criss-crossing the larger one.

Sometimes the mountain levelled out and we would get momentary respite, before we started climbing again. My thirst was now one continuous ache and my tongue felt rough and dry. Nobody spoke. Even Gift was quiet, although I could see that his eyes were open, as if he was willing us forward with his gaze.

Finally, miraculously, we rounded some big rocks, and heard a burst of wings as birds took off into the air in front of us. They flew from a ledge next to a crack in a boulder, from which a thin stream of water trickled, falling in a thin line, and disappearing into the rocks below. I heaved a huge sigh of relief.

Mother tasted the water, then said it was okay and we could drink it, though I was so thirsty I think I would have drunk it anyway.

After we had all had a long drink and splashed our hot faces, mother stripped Gift and washed him under the spring, then she dressed him and tied him to her back again and said we must continue climbing uphill.

We had not yet reached the halfway mark but mother said that we were high enough up to find a cave that could offer us protection. And we did not have to go too far before we broke through some bushes and onto a wide ledge, at the far end of which was a sheer wall of rock rising up the mountain.

Mother led us towards this wall.

Chapter 25

Whenever I've seen the Phezulu mountains from the bus on Saphela road, I've wondered what it's like on top. I imagined it would be a beautiful place, one where the Freedom Fighters used to have their camps, and where the *pungwes* were held.

But there was no time to admire the scenery. We were looking for a place to hide.

Bushes grew along the bottom of the wall of rock and big boulders lay amongst the them as if they had been pushed from the top of the mountain by a giant.

Mother said we must search for a cave or any shelter along this wall. Indeed it looked like a good place for hiding; even the countryside below was not visible, hidden as it was by vegetation.

It was Auntie who found the cave. She'd been walking in front of us and had come to a stop beside a big boulder leaning against the wall. Beside it was an opening the width of a scotch cart, but with a low roof.

'Let's take a look inside before the children go in,' mother said, as Auntie stood before the opening. 'There might be animals inside.'

I tried to look into the cave from where I was standing, but it was too dark to see inside. I knew that if I'd been with my friends, without any adults to hold us back, we would all have been inside the cave by now. We've often explored the caves in the small hills around Mbongolo village without coming to any harm.

Auntie took a stone and threw it into the cave. We heard it clattering inside, and there was a whirr of wings and bats flew out and disappeared. They were so fast they seemed like shadows of other, bigger bats flying higher up the mountain.

'Just bats,' mother said, but Auntie threw another stone into the opening. We heard it clatter into silence, and I thought that if there was a snake inside, it would only burrow deeper into the rock clefts. Then Auntie put her head inside the mouth of the cave. She was motionless for a while, her body stooped low. I imagined something inside the cave snapping her head off and her headless body falling backwards – maybe it was the headless body in the river that made me think like that, but nothing of the sort happened. Then Auntie got on her hands and knees and went into the cave and disappeared.

'Is everything okay?' mother called into the dark interior, concern in her voice.

'Wait.' Auntie's voice echoed back.

I looked at Uncle Ndoro. A task like this would normally have been undertaken by the man in the group, but Uncle Ndoro still occupied another world where he was looking for his bus. I almost thought if I had looked deep into his eyes I would find the vehicle there.

We waited for a little while. And then Auntie's head emerged from the opening.

'You can come in,' she said, 'it looks safe.'

We climbed into our new home.

***

Once we had crawled through the entrance, we found we could stand up in the middle of the cave; and once our eyes got used to the dim light, we found that we were in an uncluttered space almost the size of our kitchen at home. 'This seems fine for now,' mother said, sounding relieved. 'We can rest here and then plan our next move. Let's unpack the bag and lay our things out to dry.' A heavy fatigue settled over me now that we'd found a place that offered us safety. In fact we all looked and sounded exhausted except for Gift who was giving little explosive squeals of delight from mother's back, as if it was all an exciting adventure. At that moment, it was very easy to want to be a baby again, with no memory of all that had happened to us.

I helped Auntie to unpack the bag. We spread our wet clothes and the two blankets on the side on the cave floor. Auntie placed the radio against the cave wall. I doubted if it would still work after all the water that must have got into it during the rainstorm and in the river.

'We could dry our clothes outside,' mother said. 'But it would be very easy for someone to spot them and discover our hideout, especially if that helicopter comes this way again.'

We also took the food out of its plastic wrapping and laid it out on the rock to dry. There was only a small lump of the *inkobe* remaining, enough for one meal of a handful for each of us, but we still had the cabbage, and the lion biltong. We placed our utensils beside the food and with our possessions spread out on the cave floor, it almost looked as if we were playing 'family' with my cousins.

There seemed to be no water within sight, but the spring we had drunk from was only a short climb down the mountain, and although we had lost our container, we could fetch water from there in the pot. I wondered if we would find a spring closer to the cave. Having emptied the travelling bag, Auntie asked me to help her collect some branches to cover the mouth of the cave. We quickly cut a few from a nearby thorn bush and dragged them back to the opening.

Mother was sitting against the far wall facing the cave mouth, with Gift asleep on her lap, and Uncle Ndoro beside her.

'We can have something to eat now,' she said, 'but we have no water,'

Auntie offered to fetch some.

'We can look for water on this ledge tomorrow once we're rested,' Auntie said. She took the pot and left the cave. Mother told her to be careful.

Chapter 26

We waited for Auntie to return before we ate and I dozed off with my head against mother's shoulder. Then we had a meal of biltong sticks and raw cabbage leaves, but when Auntie offered Uncle Ndoro his portion, he did not even look at it.

'We're going to have problems with him,' mother said, looking at Uncle Ndoro. 'Leave the plate near him, perhaps when he's hungry he'll eat of his own accord.' When we'd finished, we all had a long drink of the cool mountain water from the pot, leaving a little for Uncle Ndoro, and finally we sat back to rest, my head against mother's shoulder.

'We should decide what to do in the morning,' Auntie said softly.

Darkness had descended but the moon was already floating in the sky; we could see it filtering through our protective branches, offering us a pale silver light.

We sat in silence for what seemed a very long time in the moonlit cave. Strangely, when we'd arrived, I'd felt so tired I thought I would drop, but now sleep would not come. I noticed that mother and Auntie were also awake, their eyes fixed on the mouth of the cave, as if they expected somebody to appear and tell us that everything was all right and that we could now go home.

Uncle Ndoro had folded himself into a ball in a corner of the cave and was snoring gently.

Time seemed endless and I wondered how long were we going to sit like this – tired and sleepless.

'Mama?'

'Yes?'

'The radio,'

'What of it?'

'Let's try and listen to the news, maybe the police have arrested the soldiers and we can go home.'

'The radio can't be working now Rudo, not after getting so wet.' Auntie's voice was drowsy.

I picked up the radio.

'What are you doing, Rudo?' mother snapped. 'That thing can't be working. Leave it and sit down.'

I thought mother and Auntie were right, that no radio could survive the dousing it had received, but as I was putting it back against the wall, I pushed the 'on' button by mistake and nearly fell over in shock as a loud voice suddenly filled the room. My eyes swivelled towards the mouth of the cave, as if there was a soldier standing there yelling at us.

'Rudo!' mother shouted.

I switched off the radio.

'It's working!' Auntie said in astonishment.

'Yes, we can hear that,' mother said irritably, 'but do we want to tell the whole world where we're hiding? Don't you realise there might be other people on the mountain?'

'I'm sorry, Mama.' I apologised. 'I didn't see that the volume was set at high and I didn't mean to switch it on.'

'Bring the radio here!'

Peering at it in the dim light, she set the volume to low, and then switched it on again.

We heard a voice but I did not recognise the language, though I thought it sounded like Venda.

'That's Tonga,' Auntie exclaimed. 'My ex-husband's mother is Tonga and she spoke it when her people visited us.'

'What's it saying?'

'I don't understand the language,' Auntie said. 'I can only recognise it.'

Mother tried other stations, but on one there was music, and on another a male voice was reading a story in English. Mother returned to the Tonga voice on our vernacular station, Radio Two, but just as before, we could not understand what was being said. Mother switched off the radio.

'Please don't switch it off, Mama,' I said. 'Let's wait for the news.'

'There's no news right now. We'll switch it on later. We must save the battery. I can't believe it's still alive.' Mother spoke as if the radio was a human being.

* * *

The cave began to feel very cold, but I couldn't put on a jersey or cover myself with a blanket as they were still damp and would take long to dry on the cave floor. I huddled up against mother, who had Gift on her lap, trying to share her warmth.

We relapsed into silence. Uncle Ndoro's eyes were open again.

We could no longer see the moon through the branches, and the faint light was dimmer still. Even to each other, we were now just barely visible shadows, and while it seemed to increase our sense of safety, the darkness had a ghostly feel to it.

Now and then I switched on the radio, making sure the volume was still turned down. Mother did not chastise me. The first time we heard the Tonga voice, the second time, a Michael Jackson song, the third time there was an Ndebele programme on traditional dance, and then, much later, I heard the news in English, which meant that the Shona and Ndebele news had already been read. I listened carefully but nothing was said about the soldiers in our village. I explained this to mother and Auntie.

'Maybe the police are keeping it a secret so as to catch those soldiers unawares,' Auntie suggested. 'It's impossible that our government has not heard about this with all that shooting and all those people killed. Besides, the main road runs through to Bulawayo. Is it possible that no one – *no one* – has been to the city who hadn't seen that madness?'

'If you're right, then we'll have to wait until the radio tells us something good,' mother said. 'But let's sleep now; and Rudo please don't turn on the radio again. We need to save the battery.'

With that, mother leant back against the cave wall. I could see her shadowed face, and noticed that her eyes were open. Uncle Ndoro's head had toppled onto Auntie's lap; he was snoring again. Auntie did not push him aside, as if he was her child or someone with whom she was very familiar.

***

Whenever Uncle Ndoro had visited our home, Auntie had never showed him any warmth, although she bought things from him like her skin-tight tiger dress, but now in the cave she seemed protective of him. How danger and sorrow could change people. I was happy to see this good side of Auntie. It seemed that a new and kind person had been born inside her.

It was difficult to fall asleep. I was worried like everybody else. My mind seemed to flit from frightening image to frightening image. All the events of the previous afternoon seemed to flash through my mind and with them my anxiety grew. What did the future hold for us? Would things ever be normal again? Would mother and I have to change our Shona names into Ndebele ones, so that people would not be angry with us or blame us for the murder of their relatives?

I so much wanted to turn on the radio and listen to the news. It seemed our only possible source of comfort, but remembering mother's order, I finally fell into a troubled sleep.

Chapter 27

I woke up from a terrible dream. I was swimming in the Ngwizi River, which was full. The sun was shining, making the water sparkle. Gift was on the other side of the river looking grown-up although he was still a baby; with a big smile on his face, he was clapping his hands for me. I was swimming perfectly towards him. The water was calm. Then, suddenly, a hippo surfaced and opened its huge mouth. I was swimming right towards this enormous red mouth with its big sharp teeth. They were so white, it seemed as if they had been cleaned with Colgate. I wanted to turn back and swim fast to the shore, but my hands refused to listen to me, and kept paddling me towards the mouth, which grew bigger and bigger as I drew nearer to it. Then the water was no longer still, it became a roaring flood, battering against the hippo's head as if it was a big rock. The hippo's mouth remained huge and open. Then the river was suddenly full of naked bodies without heads. They were also flowing towards the hippo's mouth, which suddenly became the mouth of a cave. The bodies all flowed into the cave, and my head flowed with them, and the cave mouth snapped shut over my neck like a mousetrap. I woke up with my heart racing. There was a sharp pain in my neck and I was lying on rock. For a moment, my mind was playing tricks: I thought I was in bed at home, and that the bed had turned to stone, which seemed somehow a part of my dream.

I could see the mouth of a cave covered with thorn branches like the fence around our maize field, and beyond it bright sunlight, but I couldn't place anything. The sunlight was dazzling my eyes, and splashing on the rocks all around me.

Then it all came back to me in a flood: I was in a cave near the top of the Phezulu mountain. We had spent all day yesterday trying to escape to this place with mother, Auntie, Gift, and Uncle Ndoro.

Then I realised that I was alone, and that the thorn branches had been partly pushed aside, leaving a small opening. I walked to the mouth of the cave, got down on my hands and knees, and crawled out through the opening.

***

I stood for a moment outside looking all around me. Now that I was outside, the sun was brighter still. Stretching away from me was the ledge of dark rock sloping gently down to the bushes, the ones we had walked through yesterday. To the left and right was more thick foliage. There was no sign of anyone. Panic was rising inside me. Where could they have gone?

Then I heard a hiss, and looking to my right saw mother. She was standing under a tree across the rock clearing with Gift peeping over her shoulder. Beside her were Auntie and Uncle Ndoro. I walked across to them.

'We left you sleeping,' mother said. 'We wanted to see where we are.'

'Let's look for some fruit to eat,' Auntie said. And with those words, hunger washed over me. Uncle Ndoro was staring sightlessly in front of him.

Chapter 28

Auntie led us deeper into the scrub. We walked parallel to the rising wall of mountain. Many trees grew here, most of them *musasa* and thorn, but bird sound quickly led us to a fig tree. Some of its fruit was ripe, and some of it had fallen like a carpet on the rock around the tree.

We began collecting it up. Birds were happily pecking at the fruit in the tree as well, so we were serenaded by their song, as if they were happy for us. Uncle Ndoro stood beside us gazing into space.

After we had picked enough fruit, we sat under the tree and had a fig breakfast, inspecting each fig closely first as they so often have maggots inside them. Auntie had pulled Uncle Ndoro down beside her, and offered him some, but he took no notice, staring in front of him as if we were not there.

'He must eat, or else he's going to starve,' mother said.

Then Auntie came up with a solution. She took a fig, broke it in half, and pressed it against Uncle Ndoro's lips: he opened his mouth, took the fruit, chewed and swallowed. Mother was breast-feeding Gift and Auntie was feeding Uncle Ndoro. I began to imagine Auntie carrying Uncle Ndoro on her back, just as mother carried Gift.

After we'd had our fill, mother said we must collect some more ripe figs, break them open and leave them to dry in the sun. As protection from squirrels and birds, we placed several thorn branches over them.

We then continued walking around the mountain and soon discovered some *umviyo*, a few of which we ate fresh, and the rest we placed beside the figs to dry. Uncle Ndoro followed close behind Auntie, almost like a pet dog, as if in her lay both his health and his sanity.

After eating so much fruit, I found I was very thirsty.

'Let me walk about a bit and search for water,' Auntie offered. 'There should be something. Maybe the source of that spring below is not too far away.'

She headed towards the bushes to the left of the rocky ledge. While we were waiting, mother said we must take some fresh figs back with us to the cave, and she took off her woolly hat, so we could put the figs in it.

Without waiting for Auntie, we began slowly making our way back to the cave.

Chapter 29

When we reached the cave, mother removed the branches covering the entrance and we crawled inside, mother first and Uncle Ndoro following. 'We will only cover the entrance at night when we sleep,' mother told us.

We emptied the fresh figs onto the plastic bag where all our food was laid out, and then sat back against the wall to wait for Auntie.

I took the radio and switched it on, but it wasn't yet time for the news, so I switched it off. Gift kept wanting to crawl towards the light at the cave mouth and mother was kept busy trying to rein him in. While mother was playing with Gift, I noticed Uncle Ndoro reach into a trouser pocket and take out a packet of cigarettes, which looked damp and crumpled. Then he reached into another pocket and took out a blue plastic lighter.

I watched him carefully, wondering if he'd recovered his mind. I hoped so much that he had because it's not a good thing to lose your mind, and I thought it'd be good to have a fully thinking man among us.

I was about to draw mother's attention towards Uncle Ndoro, but I hesitated as he pulled a cigarette out of the crumpled pack. It was broken and drooping but he put the cigarette into his mouth, back to front. He flicked the lighter and there was a spark of flame. I quickly went over and removed the cigarette from his mouth but as soon as I touched it, it broke in two, the filter fell to the ground and I was left with a tiny piece of tobacco. I had meant to put the right end of the cigarette into Uncle Ndoro's mouth.

Mother's voice snapped through the silence. 'What's burning?' An acrid smell filled the cave but the filter was lying on the ground unlit.

I explained what had happened.

Mother stepped over to Uncle Ndoro and took the cigarette pack and the lighter away from him.

'The cigarettes are damp, Uncle Ndoro,' she said soothingly. 'We will dry them for you.' Uncle Ndoro gazed straight ahead and gave no indication that he had heard her. Mother looked at me. 'Did you take the cigarettes and the lighter from his pocket for him?'

'No, I told you, he did that on his own.'

'Then he must slowly be coming to his senses.' Mother looked carefully at Uncle Ndoro's eyes. Then I saw Gift crawling towards the cave mouth, and I went and brought him back to us. He started to cry.

'Shush, shush, Gift,' mother said, clicking the lighter. Gift looked at it suspiciously and fell quiet.

Mother turned to Uncle Ndoro again.

'Uncle Ndoro?' He gave no response. Mother then carefully tore open the packet and took all the cigarettes out. Some of them were crushed, others, although soggy, were intact.

'I'm going to put these in the sun to dry, Uncle Ndoro, but I'm going to keep the lighter as we might need to use it.'

'As soon as they dry,' she told us, 'we'll give him one to smoke, maybe it will wake something in him.'

***

Auntie returned much later. We'd begun to worry if we ought to go and look for her.

'I found a spring not far from here,' she told us. 'I had a bath in it. It's just like the other spring, though slightly bigger.' She looked cleaner and fresher.

'Tell me how to get there and I'll take Rudo and Gift for a wash,' mother said.

***

The spring fell from the wall of rock at head height, and splashed on the rock before disappearing down the slope.

We took off our clothes and had a shower. Gift was the one who enjoyed it the most as he was smiling and beating the water with his hands in excitement, but I think we all felt how nice it was to be clean and cool again.

We had brought the pot with us and we filled it with fresh water. I looked up the mountain that towered over us. Above it, the sky was clear. On a distant ledge, I saw something that looked like a rock rabbit, a small isolated figure silhouetted against the blue sky, and the sight of something so normal gave me a sense of peace, as if the troubles in the village were a thing of the past.

When we returned, Auntie said she was going to take Uncle Ndoro for his bath.

'Do you think he'll be able to shower in his state?' Mother asked.

'If he doesn't, I'll help him,' Auntie told her. 'He must be clean, like the rest of us, in this small cave.'

She led Uncle Ndoro away by the hand. I noticed that he was not walking, but shuffling, and I wondered if it was because he was sick, or was just unused to exercise because he was a bus driver.

Chapter 30

Gift's smile reminded me of his father, Uncle Genesis, whose nickname around the village was Mahleka, meaning 'the one who is always laughing'. Occasionally I'd heard relatives calling Gift playfully by the same name, and I remember Uncle Genesis once saying to Gift in pretend reproach: 'What kind of a baby is this that steals the nickname of its parent?'

'You gave him that smile, Uncle Genesis,' his wife had reminded him.

Although now an old man in his seventies, Uncle Genesis had one wish: 'to go down South for the last time to get a pension.'

He had worked in South Africa for many years and married MaDube, the mother of Gift, there. MaDube was Xhosa, and they had had five children in South Africa, before Uncle Genesis had decided to return to Mbongolo at independence. When he arrived in the village with his family, he built the store at our bus stop. A year afterwards, in 1982, it was robbed by the dissidents, and a few months later it had burned down after Uncle Genesis dropped a match on some paraffin when he was trying to light a candle. Nobody had been hurt, but Uncle Genesis had given up the store. It was after that, that he began saying he wanted to work in South Africa one last time for a pension, even though he was so old. Auntie always said that this wish was just the nostalgia of an old man. And now Uncle Genesis, with his grand dream, was gone, and his smile would never light our Jamela bus stop again.

When Auntie returned, Gift cried out in fright and scuttled for mother's lap because Auntie was carrying a dead mouse in her hand, and to our surprise she had an earthen pot balanced on her head.

'I found this in a small cave next to the spring,' she said as she put it down.

I was looking at the pot suspiciously. Old and burnished, it had clearly once been used for cooking over a fire. I also knew that such pots littered the bushes and hills around our village. People used them for traditional religious purposes, and often put medicinal herbs in them before leaving them in the forest to cast away bad luck. I also knew that the proper way for that bad luck to disappear was for it to stick to somebody else, especially anyone who picked up the pot. Other people cast away their bad luck with chickens and goats and sometimes we would meet these creatures roaming freely in the bush with beads or ribbons tied to their necks or legs.

'Auntie you know you shouldn't have taken that pot.' Mother's brow was furrowed with worry.

'I washed it thoroughly,' Auntie said firmly. 'Whatever it contained cannot affect us now. The spirits will understand. We are in distress and we need it so that our children will live.'

Mother and I stared silently at the earthen vessel. It was if we expected to see smoke followed by a spirit coming out of it with a bad-luck charm that it would hurl at Auntie.

Eventually, mother shrugged her shoulders and seemed to relax, but Gift still clung to her, his fear of the dead mouse palpable. His babbling might in normal circumstances have made me laugh, but not this time.

My eyes swivelled towards Uncle Ndoro. His hair had been washed and tidied, so he now had a clean, neat line around his face.

'I found some food, too,' Auntie announced. She held up the mouse.

Mother was silent. I think she was remembering Auntie's revulsion for mice and the numerous jokes that had been made at her expense. The mouse's small head was squashed and its mouth gaped open, revealing blood on its tiny teeth.

'I hit it with a rock when we were coming back from the spring,' Auntie said. There was a faint smile on her face. 'We're going to share it if we can cook it,' she went on. 'But we don't have matches to make a fire.'

'We have Uncle Ndoro's lighter,' I said.

'Are you going to eat it?' mother asked Auntie.

'Yes we're going to eat it together, this is food isn't it?' Auntie replied.

Mother just stared at Auntie, as I did.

'I realise that I've never fully accepted you,' said Auntie. There was a sort of determination in her voice, as if she had been thinking about this for a long time, and now wanted to put it behind her. 'I'm sorry about that, Mamvura. And if my brother Innocent were here, I would tell him this too.' She looked at me, and I looked at the ground, feeling slightly embarrassed. 'It's because of my bad marriage and I've been taking it out on you.'

'It's all right,' mother said. 'But you still don't have to eat something you don't like.'

'No, I'm going to eat it,' Auntie said, and smiled. 'There's nothing wrong with mouse meat. It's an animal, just like a rabbit.'

'I'm scared, Auntie.' Mother seemed to change the subject.

'About what?'

'About what's happening. This country is for everybody: the Shona, the Ndebele, Kalanga, Venda, Tonga, Suthu and all the other tribes that live within our borders, even the whites, the Indians, the Chinese, coloureds, everybody. Isn't this why we went to war?'

'Don't worry, Mamvura,' Auntie said, and her voice was warm and comforting.

'Thank you, Auntie.' Then I heard a sob. It seemed to come from somewhere very deep, and I glanced quickly at mother. She had covered her face with her hands. Gift stretched forward in her lap and plucked at her hands with his. Mother uncovered her face. There were tears on her cheeks.

When I heard mother cry, all the sobs that I'd pushed back down inside myself seemed to want to break out of me, but when I saw Gift reaching up to mother, I managed to contain myself. The baby was indeed a blessing.

And Auntie seemed somehow much stronger. She was quick to make decisions and carry them out, just as she had been quick about ending her marriage, and chasing her former husband away from our home. Now, she called me.

'Rudo, let's go and gather firewood. We'll boil some biltong and roast this mouse. Food will keep us strong while we wait for the government to save us. They're always so slow to act when people are suffering in the villages.'

**

It was when Auntie began exchanging letters with Mr Mkandla that her attitude to men changed. Sometimes, after she had been drinking, I would hear her say to father in a sweet voice, 'Men are so good, it's only that former husband of mine who's an idiot.'

At the time, and though I was the go-between, I had only once seen Auntie and Mr Mkandla together, and it was at Belinda's home, when I saw them sharing beer from the same mug. I wondered if they loved each other, but I remembered the rumour about Miss Grant and Mr Mkandla. Could a man who has a white girlfriend also like a village woman, especially one who was not educated and had rough hands? Besides, Mr Mkandla had a beautiful wife. Of course, there are many men in the village who have more than one wife but, to be honest, Auntie just did not seem Mr Mkandla's type.

I also knew that people could write letters to each other and still just be friends, but why would they write to each other, and why did Auntie dress smartly when she went to drink beer? Of course, I couldn't discuss any of these thoughts with my friends because Auntie is my relative, but I wished I could talk to someone.

Chapter 31

We walked around searching for dry wood, which we found lying in abundance on the mountain slopes. We collected as much as we could carry, and then Auntie said, 'Time to find more meat!'

I thought she was joking, but I had wondered how we were going to divide one tiny mouse between four people. We'd seen several rock rabbits and squirrels, but I didn't see how we could catch them with our bare hands.

'How do you plan to do that?'

'There are plenty of mice around.'

'But it's difficult to catch a mouse – they're too fast.'

'Maybe I'll be lucky again.'

We headed towards the spring.

An eagle soared high in the sky, and below it, perched on a boulder, was another rock rabbit. Suddenly, the eagle swooped down and in a flash the rabbit leapt from the rock and disappeared.

We walked past a tree where monkeys screeched as they leapt from branch to branch. Then we reached the spot where Auntie said she'd killed the mouse. When we looked closely, we could see a little rodent path tunnelling through the grass. We crouched behind a boulder, and after a while, a mouse hesitantly appeared. Auntie quickly threw a stone at it, but missed, and the creature instantly disappeared into the rocks. I wished I could show Auntie the trap that father had made when he'd caught the mouse – he had made it using a flat piece of heavy rock balanced on thin sticks, but I couldn't remember exactly how he did it.

We waited with some small pebbles at hand, but finally we gave up. Then we walked back to collect the firewood, and Auntie said we must first go and look down at the countryside through which we had fled.

We walked towards the far end of the mountain ledge from where we could see the land spreading beneath us towards the horizon. I hadn't realised we were so high up. The Saphela road was very small and the Ngwizi River glinted silver on the horizon to the west. There was no sign of anyone anywhere. I wondered if other people were somewhere hiding in bush and waiting for nightfall to continue their flight under cover of darkness.

Then I felt Auntie touch my shoulder. She was pointing south.
'Look!'

I looked. I couldn't see anything at first, but as my eyes focused I saw a faint column of smoke rising, and then another and another ... They were very faint; no more than light brush strokes on the surface of the sky.

'The burning continues,' Auntie said softly. 'That is Dabulani village.'

Then, like a tiny mosquito, I saw the helicopter rise from the direction of Dabulani, a speck between two columns of smoke. I pointed this out to Auntie with a feeling of panic. I wanted to run back to the cave right away and be with mother.

'Wait a bit,' Auntie said. 'It's not coming this way.'

Indeed it was flying parallel to the mountain.

Auntie said we must hide and watch it to see what it was doing.

It was far away but quite distinct – more like a bird than a mosquito. All we could hear was its faint menacing drone. That felt strange, too, because for me the menacing voice and the music had become a physical part of the helicopter. I longed to take a stone and knock it from the sky, just as Auntie had knocked the life out of that mouse.

A shadow flitted across the land beneath the helicopter like a ghost. I wondered if there was a soldier at the door with a big gun. Then the helicopter reached the mounds of Saphela mine, and seemed to hover over them.

'Is it still moving, Rudo?' Auntie asked. 'You have better eyes than me.'

I squinted at the helicopter. 'It doesn't seem to be.'

'Let's hope it doesn't turn this way,' Auntie sighed.

As the helicopter hovered, I expected to hear an amplified voice telling people it had them surrounded. But then I remembered that the mine was disused and there was nobody there. Maybe, I reflected, the soldiers, who were strangers, didn't know this and thought that people still worked and lived there.

Then we began to see things falling from the helicopter towards one of the mounds of the mine.

'What's happening, Rudo?' Auntie asked. She shaded her eyes with a hand. 'Can you see what they're dropping, Rudo?'

I shook my head, my mind blank.

***

Just before the independence elections, helicopters and small planes used to fly over our village, dropping fliers telling people which party to vote for. The papers were easy to understand, as there weren't many words, just symbols and an X where they wanted people to put their mark. We were happy to have the papers because we could use them to go to the toilet, especially in the bush where we would normally use leaves to wipe ourselves.

But whatever that helicopter was pushing down its chute was not voting papers; the bundles seemed more solid and darker, almost like wood. But why would they throw wood into a forest full of wood? Then I thought that maybe they wanted to build a camp and were throwing down their implements and materials. I suggested this to Auntie.

'You might be right,' Auntie mused. 'If they camped there, they could stop people going from the village to the city.'

My heart sank as I thought how serious the soldiers would have to be to do this. The question that I kept asking myself was – what had the people of Saphela area done to make the soldiers so angry that they could chase them like this, as if we were the mice that Auntie and I had been hunting down? Surely they couldn't be hunting us down to eat us? Human beings do not eat each other. It is only in ghost stories meant to scare us that this happens, and this was not a story.

As we watched, the helicopter turned and flew back the way it had come. We watched it until it disappeared in the direction of Dabulani village.

Chapter 32

When we returned to the cave with the firewood, Auntie announced to mother that the burning was now in Dabulani village.

'We hope that your former husband Sibanda and his family will survive,' mother said.

'Maybe the soldiers are now not as ruthless as they were at the beginning,' Auntie responded. 'When they came to our village, they seemed very very angry, but anger cools over time.'

'If they're burning Dabulani, I wonder if this means that they've left Mbongolo?'

'How can we know? But the helicopter came from Dabulani.'

Auntie was preparing a fire as she talked. She had selected a spot in the middle of the cave, almost exactly where we have a fireplace in our kitchen at home.

'Where did you see the helicopter?'

'It seemed to come from Dabulani and hovered over Saphela Mine, where it threw things down to the earth.'

'Threw things? What things?'

'The helicopter was too far away for us to see clearly. Rudo suggested that maybe they are going to set up camp there and were bringing their equipment.'

'But if they camp there, they will come in between us and home.'

'Exactly! Perhaps they're trying to stop people moving from the villages to the city.'

'Maybe they were just dumping stuff they don't need,' I said, hearing the concern in mother's voice.

'But why go all the way to Saphela Mine to dump stuff? There are lots of places around Dabulani where they could do that.'

'We can watch to see if it returns,' Auntie said. 'Maybe we'll find out what they're trying to do.'

'But do you think we should go home now, Auntie?'

'No, I don't think so, Mamvura. Let's sleep one more night and decide what to do tomorrow.'

***

The fire was burning and mother prepared to cook the mouse. She poked a stick through its body and held it over the flames to singe its fur off. The cave soon filled with the smell of burning hair. Glancing at Uncle Ndoro, I saw a new expression in his eyes, as if he had recognised something, but it vanished just as quickly. I told mother what I'd seen, and she took the smoking mouse and held it under Uncle Ndoro's nose, but he gave no reaction.

'I think he's getting better,' Auntie declared. 'He just needs more time.'

I wondered how she could remain so strong and optimistic. Seeing the helicopter had stirred all my fear.

'I'm sure you're right,' mother said. She removed the mouse from the spit and then took our knife and scraped off its charred skin. Then she cut its stomach open and removed its entrails. Shaved and disembowelled, the mouse, always small, seemed tiny and I thought it would not even satisfy Gift's small stomach.

'When roasted it will become tinier still,' mother said. 'But if I boil it in the pot and add some biltong we could all have a little soup to eat.'

'You can boil the biltong by itself,' Auntie said. 'But let's roast the mouse.'

Mother put the lion biltong into the pot, added water, and put the pot on the fire. Then she paused, took some figs from our stock and also put them into the pot.

'I've never cooked figs before,' she said. 'But strange times call for strange ideas. I'm sure they'll taste good.'

As the pot was boiling, mother again ran the spit through the middle of the mouse, then she balanced it over two small stones over some hot coals, and we sat back and watched the mouse slowly roast.

Soon the cave was filled with the delicious smell of roasting meat. The mouse looked like a little grilled bird. We always grill birds this way if we trap any in the fields.

Auntie kept glancing at Uncle Ndoro. Mother turned the mouse several times as its body spat fat into the coals. Then she removed it from the spit and put it on a plate.

'Here, Auntie,' mother said, as she added more water into the cooking pot.

Auntie took the mouse, and she broke it into four tiny portions. Then she took the plate and went over to Uncle Ndoro. Kneeling before him, she offered him the plate.

'Here's food, Baba Uncle Ndoro. Have a piece.'

Uncle Ndoro did not respond.

'Uncle Ndoro,' Auntie called again. 'Take some food and eat, this is a delicious roasted mouse just as you eat it in your village of Chisara.'

But Uncle Ndoro stared into the distance. Auntie selected a portion and placed it on the rock at Uncle Ndoro's feet, then she rose and came over to us. She knelt before mother and offered her a piece. Mother took it without saying anything, and Auntie came to me and did the same thing. I hesitated, looking at Auntie, and wondering if this was a game, but Auntie's face was very serious.

'Take it, Rudo,' mother said. She was also dead serious.

I took a piece, and then Auntie sat beside me with the last piece. We each put some salt on our tiny portion, and ate.

'We saw another mouse and I tried to hit it with a stone and missed,' Auntie said as she chewed.

'You were even lucky to hit this one with a stone,' mother said. 'These little animals are so fast. It's easier to set a trap for them like they do at in Chisara, but I don't know how to do it. It's usually the men that set the traps.'

Mother and Auntie were talking like adults chatting over a very good meal. The mouse portion had been tiny and mine was finished in one mouthful, leaving me feeling hungrier still, and I couldn't wait for mother to dish out the soup.

Auntie took a long time to chew and swallow her piece of mouse. She seemed to be relishing every bite. At last, she stood up and went over to Uncle Ndoro. She took the meat she had left beside him and fed it to him by tearing it into two even smaller bits and putting them between his lips one after the other, while encouraging him to chew, 'Eat Uncle Ndoro, this is food from your home and it will make you feel good.'

Uncle Ndoro chewed the portion mechanically as if he was not aware of what he was doing.

Finally the biltong and the fig soup was ready. It was quite thick and mother dished it onto the plate, leaving some in the pot, which she said Auntie would feed to Uncle Ndoro. I'd never eaten boiled figs before, and they didn't taste that bad, especially with a little salt. We finished eating, and then Auntie fed her patient, who ate everything she gave him.

Then Auntie rinsed the plates and the pot with a little water, before going to sit beside Uncle Ndoro again. Mother was sitting on the other side of the cave, with Gift dozing on her lap, and I stretched out on a blanket suddenly feeling very sleepy.

Before I drifted off, a chilling thought suddenly entered my mind. Maybe seeing Auntie sitting beside Uncle Ndoro as if she was a servant waiting to serve him, and the images of her eating the mouse, something she had been against for so long, might have prompted it.

Were those soldiers doing all those horrifying things – cutting off people's hands, burning them in their homes, stripping adults naked, beating them and herding them like cattle into a pen – were they trying to turn the Ndebele people into slaves of the Shona?

Chapter 33

The days that followed were much the same. We spent them just sitting or sleeping in the cave. Sometimes we would go out to the spring to get water, or to wash. Uncle Ndoro's condition did not show any sign of improving. He remained withdrawn in his own world, only he no longer asked us about his bus.

The thought that maybe the soldiers were trying to break down the Ndebele people, had also evaporated as the more I watched Auntie helping Uncle Ndoro, the more I began to feel that she was doing it out of love, not out of fear.

On the third day, mother had taken Uncle Ndoro's cigarettes, which had long dried, and had offered him one, but he just stared at it. Auntie had lit it for him and had even smoked it a bit to show him what it was and how it was smoked, and then she had pressed it to his lips, but Uncle Ndoro just let it dangle there until it fell. Then, mother had taken the cigarettes away, saying that one day when Uncle Ndoro awoke from his sickness, he would need them.

***

The following afternoon, after spending a listless morning, we had taken turns to go to the spring to bath just as we'd been doing every day. Auntie went first with Uncle Ndoro, then mother, Gift and me afterwards.

We were returning to the cave when we heard the drone of the helicopter. It sounded far away, but mother said we must hurry to the cave and we increased our pace to a trot.

Once inside, we listened for the sound again.

'I think it's the same helicopter going to Saphela mine,' Auntie said.

'But if they're building a new campsite there, why haven't we heard the helicopter over the last few days?'

Nobody answered mother's question.

After some time the drone faded away.

Then, much later in the afternoon, we had heard it again, hovering, as if it was looking for something or dropping something.

'They must be planning something big at the mine,' Auntie said. 'I hope they don't build another prison there as well.

'I'm going to the edge of the mountain,' Auntie said, and she asked mother if I could go with her since I have better eyes than her.

Mother agreed but she was clearly very worried and asked us to be careful not to let ourselves be seen.

The sun was setting behind the mountain when we reached the edge. It cast a long, deep shadow on the country below us stretching towards the mounds of Saphela Mine, like an uneasy spirit.

'There are no signs of a new construction around Saphela Mine,' I told Auntie, after peering hard into the distance.

'I think you're right,' Auntie said. 'Let's just sit here a bit, maybe the helicopter will come back.'

We didn't have to wait long. The helicopter appeared from the direction of Dabulani village just as it had done before, and as before there was no rumba music, no loud voice. It headed straight for the mine like a bee heading for nectar.

Then it hovered over the mounds. By now the shadow of the setting sun covered the mine and we couldn't see if anything was being dropped by the helicopter. A tiny silver light kept flashing on its tail, as if it was a meter counting something.

Finally, it turned round in a huge circle and headed back towards Dabulani village.

***

On the fifth morning Auntie went with Uncle Ndoro to fetch water and found a place where okra grew. I went back with her and we collected the wild vegetable, which was very welcome. We were now only eating boiled figs as the biltong and cabbage had run out. We were all fed up with them, but they lay between us and hunger, which can kill if it bites you.

Another good thing happened that day, Auntie told us that Uncle Ndoro had washed himself, so we knew that up to then she'd been washing him.

We eat okra a lot at home as it grows plentifully in the bush behind our cattle pen, and it was an ideal addition to our menu. Mother mixed the okra and the figs and boiled them together, and the result was a greenish brown paste that we drank from cups. It filled my stomach and was refreshing, although I was beginning to dream of better food.

The following afternoon Auntie went out alone to walk around the mountain. I wanted to go with her to stretch my legs as we'd been sitting in the cave the whole morning, but mother had told me to stay behind.

'We have to limit our movement,' she said.

After Auntie had been gone for some time, I switched on the radio. Its battery was still strong as we only ever listened to the news, and when there was no news we would switch it off immediately. Still nothing had been said about the soldiers.

But today there was something. The Prime Minister had returned from Scotland the previous night.

'If he's back then that's better,' mother said, just as Auntie burst into the cave.

'Come and see!' she announced breathlessly.

Chapter 34

Auntie's agitation was infectious. I saw mother gather Gift to her bosom with one hand, her other gripped mine, as if we were getting ready to flee.

With the sun behind her, Auntie's face was in shadow.

'Come!' Auntie said again urgently. 'Soldiers!'

'No!' mother cried out. 'Please God, no!'

'They're not coming this way. They're in trucks on the road heading for our village!'

We quickly left the cave, leaving Uncle Ndoro inside.

'Bring Uncle Ndoro!' mother called out to Auntie.

'Let's leave him,' Auntie said. 'We're coming back and I don't think he'll run away.'

Auntie led the way to our look-out point. And we stared down at the Saphela road, a large cloud of dust hovered over it. Through this we could see army trucks heading up the road. I quickly counted them. There were nine.

'Finally!' I heard mother say excitedly 'It's happening!'

There was a shocked gasp from Auntie. Surprised, I looked at her.

'What do you mean, Rudo's mother? Those soldiers are going to kill more people!'

But mother took Auntie's hand. 'The Prime Minister has returned home!' mother told her. She was almost dancing on her feet. Tears streamed down her cheeks. 'Tell her, Rudo, tell Auntie what the radio said.'

I realised then what mother had deduced and a sense of relief washed over me.

I looked at Auntie, who was still visibly angry, and nodded my head.

'Yes, the news said the Prime Minister has come back to the country from Scotland.' I wondered if maybe their leader had heard that Miss Grant had been killed by these soldiers – after all, she was Scottish – and had told our Prime Minister to rush back to do something about it.

'We might as well collect our things and go down the mountain now,' mother said. 'It's game over for those killer soldiers.' She was wiping her eyes. 'They're going to pay heavily for the pain they have caused in the villages.'

I was the first to hear the sound of the helicopter and I tapped mother on the arm and pointed to the sky.

'I can hear it, too,' mother said. 'But where's it coming from?'

Our eyes turned towards Dabulani village, but there was no sign of the helicopter.

'Quickly, let's hide,' mother said, pointing at a bush with thick foliage. 'If it's the same people, they might shoot at us.'

We scrambled under the bushes. From my hiding place, I had a clear view of the countryside.

Then, with a deafening roar, a helicopter flashed over us from behind the mountain, taking us completely by surprise. Bulawayo city lay behind the mountain. I looked up and another helicopter thundered after the first one. Then another. All three were flying in the direction of our village just as the trucks below were, and they were all flying fast.

We were silent as we watched them. They seemed to be chasing after the trucks. I didn't know what to think, but my first idea was that we were going to witness a fight between the trucks and the helicopters – it was all so confusing.

Then the helicopters thundered over the trucks without pausing.

'They are new helicopters,' I heard Auntie say. 'They don't belong to the enemy.'

The helicopters appeared motionless as they flew towards the horizon, growing smaller and smaller.

'Good,' mother said. 'Good. There is law in this country.'

Auntie struggled out from underneath the bush, and we all followed suit. The trucks, now just small dots, were still on the road. We found some rocks and sat on them, with the countryside in front of us like a picture. We sat there for the rest of the afternoon, just watching the trucks until they finally disappeared from view, leaving behind a haze of dust floating on the horizon.

When we finally returned to the cave the sun had set and a great shadow fell over the mine like a pall.

Chapter 35

The following morning, Auntie was not in the cave with Uncle Ndoro when I woke up.

'She's taken him to watch the road,' mother told me. 'The fresh air will be good for him.'

'Do you think he'll ever recover his mind?'

'Good question,' mother replied. 'But I don't know, as I've never seen anything like this before. I think he needs to go to hospital where doctors can examine him.'

We'd been on the mountain for almost a week, but now that we thought the army had gone to the village to sort things out, a weight seemed to have been lifted from our hearts, and I could feel it. I noticed that I was not dwelling so much on our safety, but thinking more about father. I could only think of him as alive. Sometimes my mind flashed to the moments when I had seen him: a man with the sack covering his head and his hands tied to his sides with rope, huddled in the back of the army truck, and a naked man with a flaming torch in his hand being driven to burn down his home.

I also thought about how we would have to start rebuilding our home again once we'd found him.

'I know we're going to find father when we go back.' I was sitting beside mother. Gift was trying to chew on a fig and my thoughts drifted to Sithabile. My mind kept saying that we would find her alive as well, with Belinda and Nobuhle; and that she would come and live with us since she no longer had a home or a family. I wanted us to walk together to school again.

'I hope so too,' mother replied. 'But we must be very careful. We cannot go down the mountain until we're quite sure that everything is all right, or we might be killed by fleeing soldiers.'

I wondered what the village would be like, with most homes burned down and so many people killed. I wondered if there were any homes that had not been burned down, and whose homes those were. I remembered Auntie saying the clinic had also been burnt down, and I wondered how sick people could be treated without a clinic in the village. I remembered that the teachers had run away too, and I wondered if both Mbongolo Primary and Godlwayo Secondary were still standing, or had also been reduced to heaps of smoking rubble.

Then a shadow filled the mouth of the cave. It was Auntie. She crawled into the cave.

'I have brought some people with me,' her voice half abrupt, half teasing.

I saw mother's body stiffen.

'Who are they?' she whispered. 'And where is Uncle Ndoro?'

'Uncle Ndoro is outside the cave with the people I've just mentioned.'

'But who are they, Auntie?'

'The three teachers from Rudo's school. Those we glimpsed before.'

'Where are they coming from?'

'They say they've been on the mountain for the past week, but moved yesterday when they saw the army trucks going towards the village.' Auntie fell silent for a moment.

'They say the new soldiers and those in the village are one group, and they've all been sent by the government.'

'No!' mother cried out. 'That can't be!'

'The teachers know the full story.'

'Where are the teachers?'

'I left them in the bushes outside,' Auntie pointed. 'Mr Mkandla says he knows this cave and they want to come in with us.' She paused. 'But they're still naked, and we have a child here.'

Now it was mother's turn to fall silent.

'But how can they come in with us if they're naked?'

Another shadow suddenly appeared at the cave mouth. I couldn't see beyond Auntie, but I heard a voice I clearly recognised.

'We're waiting for you, MaJamela,' the voice said. 'It's dangerous out here. The helicopters might return.' The voice was gruff. It was Mr Mkandla.

'Please do not come in yet,' Auntie replied, looking over her shoulder. 'I told you that we've children in here, didn't I?'

'Please hurry up.'

'I told you to wait. Go back and hide in some bushes until I come.'

We heard the sound of footsteps retreating.

***

'What do you want us to do Auntie?' Mother's voice sounded uncertain. Gift had crawled onto her lap.

'They want to come into the cave,' Auntie said.

'We can move and look for another cave higher up if they want to come into this one,' mother said. 'There should be other caves around here.' She placed a hand on my shoulders.

'We're not moving out,' Auntie said.

'But you said the teachers want to come in here.'

'We'll stay with them.'

'But you said they're still naked, and we have a child with us, a girl.' Mother nodded her head at me. She still had her hand on my shoulders. Gift was pointing a finger at me and murmuring softly.

I sensed this was not the real reason mother wanted us to leave the cave. It was in her voice. The teachers were all Ndebele and I understood her fear. I know what revenge is all about; we often play revenge games at school. If someone hurts you, you hurt them just as they've hurt you.

'I've an idea,' Auntie said. 'We have three dresses in the bag.'

Mother fell silent.

'Okay,' she said at last.

Auntie took our travelling bag and left the cave.

***

A while later, she crawled back into the cave, leading Uncle Ndoro

126

by the hand. Behind him crawled my three teachers. Once inside the cave, they all stood up.

The Headmaster, Mr Ndlovu, was dressed in mother's blue dress, the one with the big tear, which exposed the side of his knee. The dress was too long, so he had tied it round the waist with some bark, pulling it up so that it did not drag on the floor. Although Mr Ndlovu is short, he has a portly body and the dress made him look as if he was pregnant. I had to turn my face away to stop from laughing.

Next came Mr Mkandla. He is man of medium height with strong wide shoulders. He was dressed in Auntie's tiger dress, which hugged his body, showing off his muscular chest and legs. Then came Mr Bhebhe, the geography teacher. He was in mother's brown dress with white frills. The dress looked like an oversized sack as it drooped over his slight body. Whilst the first two teachers are from other districts, Mr Bhebhe, who is about my father's age, is from Godlwayo village. All the men were barefooted.

With the men now in the cave, the space inside suddenly seemed very small. None of them made eye contact with us, as if the dresses embarrassed them, which I understood – these are respected men in the village. They sat down on the far side to the right of the cave mouth. The polished looks and confidence the teachers exuded when they were at school was history.

I looked at mother. She was busy stirring the pot on the fire with a stick, and her eyes were fixed on her task.

'Hallo, Mamvura,' Ndlovu said in a soft voice, like that of an old man who has lost something very dear to him.

'How are you, Mr Ndlovu?' mother replied respectfully, her eyes on the fire. Normally, our parents do not look teachers straight in the eye, as they are very important people, but today mother had another reason for not looking at Mr Ndlovu: my headmaster was dressed in her old dress, the one she wore when she went to work in the fields.

Then there was silence. I looked at Auntie. Her eyes were fixed on the fire, too. I quickly glanced at Mr Mkandla. His eyes were on his knees. All the men were sitting like women with their feet folded underneath them, just as we do so as not to show our panties.

The silence continued. Then mother took the pot off the fire and poured the figs and okra paste into two plates and into both of our cups.

'What's that?' Mr Ndlovu asked.

'It's our food,' Auntie replied.

'What is it?'

'Boiled figs mixed with okra,' Auntie said. 'That's all we've found on the mountain. There are mice and rabbits but we couldn't catch those.'

'We don't eat mice,' Mr Mkandla said. 'That is for Shona people.'

A silence that felt almost solid descended on the room. I noticed mother freeze.

Then mother handed the pot to Auntie.

'Give our visitors some food,' mother said to her. 'Maybe they're hungry. They can eat from the pot. There is a little left inside.'

'Would you like to try some?' Auntie asked.

'We've not eaten properly ever since we ran away from the school,' Mr Ndlovu replied. He seemed to be the spokesperson. 'We've been surviving on figs and water. We ate the figs straight from the tree. Anything cooked will do.'

'This is little,' Auntie said. 'But after you have eaten this, we can prepare more for you. We have one spoon and you can use it to spoon the food into your hands.'

Auntie lifted the gourd of water and helped the men to wash their hands by pouring for them.

Then we all had our lunch. I ate from my cup whilst mother and Auntie each ate from a plate. Auntie would feed Uncle Ndoro from the other cup after she'd eaten.

I watched the men as they ate. They each scooped the paste into their hands, and then ate the handful and then passed the spoon on to the next man. They were eating hungrily like people who have not eaten for a very long time. We, at least, were lucky to have brought a cooking pot with us, and Uncle Ndoro had inadvertently provided us with the means of fire.

***

The men finished with their food in an instant. Auntie then took the pot and filled it with more okra and figs from our store and started boiling them again for a second meal.

Then Mr Ndlovu began asking what had happened to us and how we found ourselves in the cave. Auntie related our story, how Uncle Genesis and Uncle Francis and their families had been burned to death, and how we had discovered Gift; how my father had been captured by the soldiers, and how we had fled the village, crossed the flooded river, and found Uncle Ndoro in his concussed state; and then how he'd nearly been shot by the soldiers, and how finally we had ended up in this cave on the mountain.

'It was almost the same with us,' Mr Ndlovu said. 'The soldiers just appeared at the school after all the students had left for the day – a whole truck of them led by a soldier wearing large spectacles who called himself Comrade Finish.'

'We saw that man too,' Auntie said.

'They assembled all the teachers in one classroom, and had all of us strip naked.' Ndlovu paused and shook his head. 'Then they gave one of the teachers, Mr Dube, a stick and told him to beat all of us with it. Mr Dube refused and they instantly shot him dead.' Mr Dube had been our religious education teacher.

Mr Ndlovu continued with his story. 'Then one of the soldiers took the stick and he beat all of us heavily. After that they took us to the primary school in Mbongolo where they had made a jail of barbed-wire fencing, which was filled with naked people. That is where I saw Rudo's father.'

I heard mother's breath catch. 'You saw him?' She leant towards Mr Ndlovu, but it was Mr Bhebhe who replied.

'I saw him too. He was with a group that was being forced to dig mass graves for all the people they were shooting.'

'Do you think he's still alive?' Auntie asked.

'I wouldn't know,' Mr Bhebhe shook his head sorrowfully. 'For on that first evening, we broke through the fence and escaped. Many people did, but I don't know if Rudo's father was among them.'

'We escaped with him,' Mr Ndlovu said. 'We were with a group of people, and we were all running south.

'And then what happened?'

'We hadn't gone far when Jamela suddenly said that he was going back to his home to look for his family, meaning you, and he left us and went back towards Mbongolo village.'

'We saw him,' Auntie said. 'He came to our home with the soldiers while we were hiding. We saw the soldiers beat him up and force him to burn down our home.'

'Then he must have been recaptured,' Mr Ndlovu said sadly.

A heavy silence fell. I wanted to cry. I had so much wanted to believe that father had escaped from the camp after the soldiers had come with him to our home, and not before. I clung to a hope that there been another prison-break, though I knew it was foolish. The soldiers would not let people escape twice.

'We hope the soldiers have given him another job in the camp,' Auntie said. 'That's the only thing that can keep him safe.'

'You don't know about the other jobs they're giving people in that camp.' Mr Mkandla's voice was bitter.

'What do they have to do?' Auntie asked.

'They are making neighbours kill neighbours,' Mkandla said flatly. 'They are forcing men to rape their neighbours' wives with their children watching.'

Auntie subsided into silence.

Mr Ndlovu shook his head, and took up his story. 'When we escaped, we ran in a group as teachers of Godlwayo High amongst the other people. It seemed safer to keep together; but poor Miss Grant was shot in the back as we made the break, but we managed to carry her away with us. The soldiers had raped her, too. At first we wanted to escape across the border to Botswana, but there were too many people heading that way, so we were easy to pick out. Then the helicopter started shooting at those who were fleeing, so we changed direction and left the main group. We crossed the river and headed this way. We wanted to cross the mountain and try to reach Bulawayo.'

He paused, as if reliving their flight, and then went on.

'After we'd changed direction, we did not meet a single person. It was so strange.'

'We didn't meet anyone either until we reached here,' Auntie added. 'Well, except for Uncle Ndoro, and a few dead people.'

With their heads cut off, I almost added.

'We were taking turns to carry Miss Grant,' Mr Ndlovu went on. 'But she had lost a lot of blood and died in a clearing after we'd crossed the river.'

'We were following behind you and saw her body,' Auntie said. She was now feeding Uncle Ndoro from the cup with a spoon.

'We couldn't bury her.' There was grief in Mr Ndlovu's voice. 'We wanted to, she was one of us, but there was no time. God forgive us. We just left her in the open for animals. Just like that, and after she had volunteered to come all the way from Scotland to give our children knowledge. What more kindness do you want in a person?'

I looked at Mr Mkandla. He had been Miss Grant's friend but he was looking out of the cave, his face inscrutable. He seemed to be muttering to himself, but I couldn't make out the words.

Mr Ndlovu stopped speaking and silence descended on us again as we each remembered the terrible things that we would now never be able to forget. Then he continued.

'We walked in this direction, but when we reached the mountain we continued on. We wanted to get to Bulawayo. But we soon discovered that the way to the city was blocked by soldiers, so we turned and walked back to the mountain. We were camping a little lower down, near a spring. There was no cave, only a small ledge, and we had to hide under overhanging rocks, Then, yesterday, we saw more army trucks coming into the village, and the three helicopters, and Mr Bhebhe suddenly remembered this cave, which is when we decided to climb higher up the mountain.'

'During the war we used to pass this cave on our way to the mountain-top to attend the *pungwes* with Rudo's father and other villagers,' Mr Bhebhe interjected. 'I remember it because of the spring on this level.'

'There's a helicopter which goes to and from Saphela Mine,' Auntie said.

'It's dropping dead people down the mine-shafts,' Mr Mkandla said, his voice hard and flat. 'We could see them clearly from where we were camped.'

'Oh my lord!' Mother put her head in her hands, as if this last piece of information was simply more than she could bear. 'Whatever's happening?' she whispered. 'Soldiers? Behaving like this? And why is the government allowing it to happen?'

'Are you telling us you don't know what's happening?' Mkandla's voice was curt.

'We know that the soldiers have been killing people,' Auntie said. 'They've killed all our relatives. But,' she added, 'I don't like your tone, Mkandla.'

Mr Mkandla pointed at mother. 'Her people are killing our people with the permission of the Prime Minister.' He spat his words out, as he had been holding them in his mouth like poison. '*She* must leave this cave at once.'

'She has no part in any of it,' Auntie replied. 'This is my brother's wife and she is *my* family.'

'She must get out! I don't want to be anywhere near her!' There was a dangerous note in Mr Mkandla's voice, like a snarl.

'No, Mkandla, relax please,' Mr Ndlovu said very quietly.

'Relax? Relax? You're mad! How can I relax when Shona soldiers are killing our defenceless families?'

'It's not the Shona people who are doing this, Mkandla,' Mr Ndlovu said in tired voice, as if he'd had this argument more than once. 'It's the soldiers who are doing it.'

'Do you hear what you're saying?' Mkandla blazed. 'So, today, soldiers are not *people*?'

'Okay, we'll leave,' mother said. My eyes were swimming with tears.

'They found us here,' Auntie said. 'This is our cave. We let them in.'

Mr Mkandla leapt to his feet. He had picked up a stick from our firewood pile.

'Get out before I kill you!' He was shouting, pointing the stick at mother.

'Then give us back our dresses now. We're going!' Auntie shouted back. She was also standing. 'Take off our dresses, right now!'

Mr Ndlovu stepped between Auntie and Mr Mkandla. 'Please, please, sit down all of you, please.' His voice was imploring.

But now anger gripped Auntie. She pointed a finger at Mr Mkandla's face. 'How can you do this to me?'

'Do *what?*'

'You know what I'm talking about! I've been your girlfriend!'

'What has that got to do with anything? What I said is that I do not want a Shona person anywhere near me *ever* again!'

Mother stood up. She hitched Gift onto her back, and tied him there with a towel. He had begun to cry. Then she took our bag with its few remaining clothes, grabbed my hand and half-pushed half-led me out of the cave.

Chapter 36

We headed quickly for the bushes and then mother stopped.

'Where are we going to?' I asked. I felt very weak and tearful. Rain clouds had collected in the sky, and a cool wind was blowing.

'Let's wait here for Auntie and Uncle Ndoro,' mother said quietly. Her voice had the confidence of conviction and it comforted me. We had a clear view of the cave in front of us. Angry voices carried across the clearing. Then Auntie burst out of the cave, leading Uncle Ndoro by the hand. She stopped outside the cave and looked around as if she was bewildered by the light. Mother waved at her. Auntie led Uncle Ndoro over to us.

'Look after Uncle Ndoro,' Auntie said when she reached us. 'I'm going back to get our dresses. I want to teach that Mkandla a lesson! I'm not a person to be played around with.'

'Bring our pots and plates too, we'll need them,' mother said. 'And please be careful.'

We could see Mr Ndlovu standing at the cave mouth, looking around as if he was searching for us. Auntie hesitated for a moment, and that's what saved her.

There was a short burst of gunfire, and Mr Ndlovu seemed to move for a moment like a dancing woman, and then he toppled back and disappeared.

***

'Get down!' mother whispered urgently, pushing me to the ground.

We all lay down flat. Auntie was at my side. Then I heard a noise and looked up. Uncle Ndoro had got up and was walking across the clearing towards the cave.

Nobody said anything, but our hearts were in our mouths. As we watched Uncle Ndoro, a figure appeared at the mouth of the cave. It was Mr Mkandla. He was still carrying the stick with which he had threatened mother, but he was preparing to run. The gun roared again. Mr Mkandla's body jerked and toppled to the ground, and so did Uncle Ndoro's. Then a terrible silence fell. It seemed as if the whole world had gone quiet. Not a bird sang, and mercifully Gift had not cried. I suppose he was too shocked. We waited, not knowing what we were waiting for.

After what seemed like an eternity, Auntie pointed towards a passage between two rocks and she scuttled towards them on all fours. Mother gave me a push and I followed Auntie, but not before I was sure that mother was following me. Auntie disappeared into the passage, and I followed after her. The cleavage was narrow and the rocks rubbed against our bodies. Then abruptly the passage turned, and Auntie disappeared. Turning just as suddenly, I felt the ground under my hands give away, and I screamed.

* * *

I was hanging in space. I could see the countryside below, although the land seemed to swing. Something very tight gripped my ankle. I could also see the ribbon of Saphela road. A tiny army truck parked in the bush came into view, and then it disappeared again. I was terrified.

Then the force around my ankle began to pull. My hands found purchase on the rocks, and I crawled slowly backwards grazing my knees and my shins. Someone was pulling me hard, too hard. I could not crawl fast enough.

'Come, Rudo,' mother crooned. I looked back. She was crouched low in the passage we had been fleeing through. Gift's head appeared over her back, his eyes wide with fear and incomprehension.

I crawled back into safety. Then the realisation of what had happened descended on me. A tight ball formed at the bottom of my throat, and a scream wanted to tear out of my mouth, but mother pulled me to her bosom and held me tight. Auntie!

'Don't cry, my child,' mother was murmuring to me. 'Don't cry, Rudo. Auntie has gone to rest.'

'You can come out of there now!' A male voice shouted into the passage. The voice was familiar, and he was speaking Shona.

Chapter 37

We stood at the edge of the clearing in front of the mouth of our cave. On the clearing stood five soldiers. Comrade Finish, who stood beside us, was the fifth soldier in the group. He was the one who had shouted at us.

Uncle Ndoro's body lay in the middle of the clearing, that of Mr Mkandla at the mouth of the cave. Blood flowed from both bodies like two red rivers down the rock until it disappeared into the bush at the edge of the clearing.

'There is someone inside that cave and they will not come out,' Comrade Finish said. He was addressing mother. 'I do not want my men to go in there. So what are we expected to do?' Looking at Comrade Finish, at his smart uniform with the badges on it, and his large spectacles, it was hard to believe that he was the man who was responsible for all the killing and death we had seen in the village, and now here on the mountain-top.

Mother did not reply.

'I remember you clearly,' Comrade Finish said to mother. He took off his glasses, blew on them, and then took a handkerchief and slowly wiped the lenses as if he had all the time in the world. He held the glasses up to the sun and squinted at them. Then he wiped the lenses one last time and put his spectacles on again. He looked at mother. 'We took your husband from your home and told you to escape a week ago. I have a very good memory, although I have forgotten your name.

What is it again?'

'Mamvura,' mother replied in a low voice.

'Correct,' the soldier said. 'I remember it clearly. And you are also from Chisara, so you told me. I know Chisara, I pass by it when going to my home.'

It was hard to believe that this man knew where mother's rural home was. But he did not say the name of his home, or his family name. Comrade Finish turned to me. 'I remember you, too. You said your name is Rudo.'

I did not reply. Gift, behind mother's back, kept trying to pull my ear, and I took his little hand in mine.

'Is this your daughter?' the soldier asked mother.

'Yes.'

'And the baby?'

'He is mine too.'

'What is his name?'

'He is Anovona.'

'What a good name,' Comrade Finish said. 'The one who sees all. It's good he has seen what we do to dissidents. Maybe, one day, he will become one of our brave soldiers who will help to keep our country clean of weeds and trash. It was lucky we saw those naked men climbing up the mountain, otherwise we wouldn't have freed you from their infection.'

Comrade Finish raised his hand at the men in the clearing, and they immediately advanced to the mouth of the cave; but instead of going into it, they pressed their bodies to the sides of the cave mouth.

Beside us was a huge boulder.

'Move behind the boulder, please,' Captain Finish ordered us casually, as if it was the most natural thing to do in the world. We moved behind it with him.

There was a deep, mind-numbing explosion. It seemed to come from the heart of the mountain. It echoed around us, as if there were other explosions now blasting out. I found myself tightly held in mother's hands. Gift began to scream. I could see the mouth of Captain Finish moving, although I could not hear what he was saying. Captain Finish moved around the boulder, and we followed him.

The other soldiers now stood before the mouth of the cave. Smoke was coming out of it. Then two of the soldiers went into the cave, and they came out a moment later. I had regained my hearing.

One of the soldiers looked at Comrade Finish and nodded his head. Comrade Finish turned to mother.

'Do you know anyone in the city?' he asked her.

'My husband has a house there.'

'Good, then you have a place we can take you to. We are also going to the city for a day or two to get some rest. And make sure you don't come back here – next time we won't be so lenient. We're on national duty and we don't want anything to disturb us, not even our fellow tribespeople or their children.'

***

It did not take us long to climb down the mountain. We walked in silence.

When we reached the bottom, we saw an army truck parked in the bushes.

Two soldiers were standing beside the truck.

My eyes were searching around, hoping I would spot Auntie's body, when one of the soldiers addressed the Captain.

'A woman fell down the mountain into those bushes up there,' the soldier said, pointing up at the mountain. 'And I went up and brought her down.'

I knew it was Auntie. It could not be anyone else. I tensed, expecting to see her dead body any minute.

'Where is she?' Captain Finish asked.

'In the back of the truck. She's alive, but something's wrong with her head.'

***

The soldiers made us climb on to the back of the truck, and I saw Auntie. She was sitting with her back against the cab, a huge graze down the side of her face.

'Auntie?' Mother reached out her hand to stroke her.

But Auntie did not reply. She was staring blankly at nothing. The expression in her eyes was similar to that in Uncle Ndoro's eyes, unfocused. As I looked, Auntie's lips started moving, but no words came out of her mouth.

'She has become ill,' mother whispered. 'It's the fall from the mountain, but thank God she's still alive.' Mother spoke in Shona. Perhaps she hoped that the soldiers would think Auntie was Shona, too.

* * *

She sat between us, and I held her limp hand. The soldiers were just a row of grim faces under red berets, three on either side of us. My eyes moved past their faces to the brown dust cloud that chased after the truck as it sped along Saphela road towards Bulawayo. As I looked at the dust cloud, it suddenly took the shape of father's face. I closed my eyes and pressed myself against mother, and I felt Gift's hand on my shoulder. Something told me were going to see father again, one day: if not in this life, then maybe in another.